B E S T
B L A C K
WOMEN'S
EROTICA

BEST BLACK WOMEN'S EROTICA

Edited by

Blanche Richardson

CLEIS
PRESS

Published in the United States by Cleis Press Inc.,
P.O. Box 14684, San Francisco, California 94114.
Printed in the United States.
Cover design: Scott Idleman
Text design: Karen Quigg
Logo art: Juana Alicia
First Edition.
10 9 8 7 6 5 4 3 2 1

"sex hall" by MR Daniel originally appeared in *Best Lesbian Erotica 2001*, edited by Tristan Taormino, Cleis Press, 2001. "That's What Friends Are For" by Nilaja A. Montgomery originally appeared in *Pillow Talk II*, edited by Lesléa Newman, Alyson Publication, 2000.

To my mother, Dr. Raye G. Richardson
who continues to teach me how to love myself.
And to my father, Dr. Julian Richardson—the greatest
lover of Black women I have ever known—who
taught me that I am lovable.

Acknowledgments

Thank you Cleis Press—Frédérique, Felice and Don—for trusting me with this project. Thank you for your support, your expertise, your love and your patience.

Thanks to The Marcus Books Reading Club for all the cheerleading, for your support and mostly for the friendship. You all are the best! Thanks also to my customers who have been so supportively enthusiastic about this book. I love and appreciate each and every one of you.

To the staff of Marcus Book Stores—my family—for allowing me the time to work on this project. Thank you Karen, thank you Billy, thank you Tamiko, thank you "Face," thank you Donald Ray Young, thank you Roxanne, thank you Nikki, thank you Carolyn, and thank you James.

I am truly blessed to have my writer friends who have encouraged me, supported me, pushed me to write, shared their expertise, been my best friends and loved me unconditionally. Thank you Terry McMillan, Tina McElroy Ansa, E. Lynn Harris, Tananarive Due, Iyanla Vanzant, Paula Woods, and Felix Liddell.

For keeping me grounded, I thank my grandchildren, Hank and D'Asia. You may now collect on all the personal time I owe you.

For keeping me working when I whined and complained by telling me to "get back to the mine, Shine, there'll be no strike today," I owe my sanity to my mother Raye who supported, loved, cooked for me and taught me, from the cradle, the beauty of the written word. I am so very proud to be your daughter.

And to Cherysse—for *everything*.

TABLE OF CONTENTS

Introduction

Iyanla Vanzant

I don't know about you, but my body parts have names. My hands I call "Fric and Frac." My legs are known as "Sticks and Bones." My breasts I refer to as "Gussie and Gertie." My behind is affectionately known as "Waelene." The fact that she isn't doesn't really matter. Then there's "Molly." Every woman has a Molly. Sometimes she's called "Puntang." Others may call her "Bubbles." When I first heard someone refer to her as "Vagina," I had no idea who or what she was talking about.

"You mean 'Virginia,' don't you?"

"No!" my classmate responded emphatically, "It's called a vagina. V-a-g-i-n-a. That's the proper name for it."

Rather impersonal, don't you think? Then again, many women, particularly Black women, have a very impersonal relationship with their "M-o-l-l-y." It's a historical thang.

My grandmother, coming from the South and growing up in the church like she did, only knew Molly to be a betrayer. Based on her experiences as a sharecropper's daughter, Molly was someone who could be used against you. Her Molly, no doubt, was a source of sin and shame. Once she even told me that her mother, my great-grandmother, had been raped repeatedly by a group of lumberjacks. So brutal was the attack, my great-granny was unable to walk for weeks. The fact that she eventually went on to have six children was both blessing and curse. "She died," Grandma said, "at the age of thirty-two from some dreaded disease *down there.*" She remembered her mother as a soft-spoken, kind-hearted woman who had died too early, leaving six children under the age of ten. To my grandma, Molly was a thief who had robbed her of a mother. In essence, Molly was a problem.

My mother never talked to me about sex. She was a proud woman of Caribbean heritage who honestly believed that women were subservient to men. Women, and their body parts, had two main purposes: 1) to work hard; and 2) to serve and satisfy men. My mother never talked to me about the pleasures or the intricacies of an intimate sexual experience. She never told me that sexual activity was good for my health. Nor did she tell me about the beautiful experiences of sexual exploration—with self or with others. "Don't worry about such things," she said. "When you need to know, you will know." In fact, to women of my mother's generation, expressions of sexuality and the notion of a woman's sexual identity were dirty. What momma did do was warn me. She warned me never to display Molly publicly. She warned me about all the trouble Molly could get me into if I allowed people to touch her or talk to her. She went so far as to warn me about sitting on men's laps, telling me that I could catch something—like pregnancy. "That's silly!" I thought. Still, I made it a point never to *sit* on men. Instead, I lay down with them.

Molly had a name, but she and I were not actually connected. She was not connected to my hands, my legs, my breasts, or my heart. Somehow, grandma's stories and momma's stories had infiltrated my head. There was a slight disconnect between Molly and the rest of my body. Many times, Molly caused me pain and shame. I got *caught* doing things with Molly that momma had warned me not to do. Many times, Molly made alliances that caused my heart grief. It always seemed that the people she liked didn't like her back. After Molly had fostered the birth of three children, she lost her youthfulness, her playfulness. Her response time was slower. Some of her associates even commented on her size. They couldn't get close to her, they said. She was not as affectionate as they thought she should be. Molly did her best, but, I finally realized, she had changed. She had matured. She was run-down, not feeling good about herself. We had a talk, Molly and I. That's when I decided to change her name to "Mabel." It seemed to more appropriately describe her state of being. Stately. Soft spoken. Useful, but somewhat removed from the fullness of her nature.

As women, so many of us are deprived of a healthy respect of and connection to our sexuality. For some, it is shrouded in so much shame by so many convoluted messages that we actually become detached from our sexual identities. We like sex, but we can't talk about it. We engage in sex, but we are, at times, afraid to enjoy it. When we do enjoy the act, and our partners, we are often subjected to ridicule and heartbreak. It can get confusing and tiring. How can something so good be bad for you? How can something that feels so good cause so much pain? It's a question that we still ask ourselves today. Fortunately, however, we are talking more about it.

As women, we are exploring our sexuality and exhibiting our sexual identity from a more integrated perspective. We've got our heads involved now. We are thinking about what we are doing. We've got our hearts involved now. We are not allowing feelings to drive us or deprive us. We are talking more now, about our Mollys and Mabels. We are sharing and comparing notes on how to care for this part of ourselves.

How to preserve this aspect of our beings and bodies. How to satisfy our needs as an expression of, and with respect for, who we are as women. We no longer hide our sexuality. Instead, we are exploring and defining it, privately and publicly. We are no longer willing to accept our sexual identity as a "dependent appendage." We no longer limit sexuality to our body parts. We are discovering our sexual nature to be a source of creativity. A wellspring of our health, and a source of pleasure for which we are now willing to accept full responsibility in manifestng. Mabel has come into her fullness. She is now known in a very private arena as "Peaches and Cream." She is not just a "Lunchable," she's a full course meal!

As you move through the pages of this book, do not just read the words; feel them. Undoubtedly, they will trigger your own memories of some stories you've been told that you may want to rewrite. The stories you will read here may evoke uncomfortable feelings that you may need to come to grips with on your own journey to a deeper understanding and greater appreciation of our sexual identity and nature. From a more practical aspect, you may want to consider that the fullness of sexual expression as orgasm drains your lymph nodes. In women, lymph nodes are actively involved in several forms of cancer. You may not be aware that the enzymes released throughout your body at the height of sexual arousal lubricate your skin. You may find it interesting that the same number of calories you burn with one good, thirty-second orgasm, would take twenty minutes to burn on a treadmill. If that's not enough to convince you that erotic activity and thoughts are good for you, how about the plain old truth that it's pleasurable! It's fun! Most of all, it's private. For all the years of service to others, don't you and Molly or Mabel or Peaches— or V-a-g-i-n-a—deserve to have a little fun? Why not relax and enjoy? You'll feel a lot better.

Do Me
Lori Bryant-Woolridge

There is nothing worse than to be awakened from a great sleep for no apparent reason. I lay there in the dark, refusing to open my eyes, hoping like hell that my mind and body would take the hint and go back to sleep. After thirty-five minutes and countless tosses and turns, I gave up, sat up, switched on the bedside lamp, and tried to get my bearings straight.

I was here in Aruba, a four-hour plane ride from my cozy little New York apartment, finishing up preproduction chores for the new music video by Keisha, the latest rage in the young, uni-moniker (think Aaliyah, Monica, Brandy), R & B chart busters. My job as a producer at SunFire Productions was to help make these nymphet divas (and their male counterparts) as saleable as possible. It was a tough job, but one I still adored after nearly eight years.

I glanced over at the clock and noted with a groan that it was only 6:47 a.m. I was supposed to check out Malmock Beach in the late-morning light, which gave me at least another three hours of sleep—if only my mind would cooperate with my travel-weary body. But it was soon clear that it wouldn't, so I reached over and grabbed the stack of magazines I'd brought with me.

I quickly breezed through the always-entertaining *Jet* before taking on *Essence,* where I learned that it was indeed possible to love both God and sex. Thank goodness for that bit of heartening news. Several pages apart was a lovely pictorial of bridal gowns that promised to "satisfy the soul." Seemed to me that there was nothing a wedding dress could do for my soul that God and/or sex couldn't do better. Then again, being thirty-six years old and single, I wouldn't know.

Moving on, I picked up the latest *Elle* and flipped through eighty pages of advertisements before finding anything to read. Uninterested in the return of the '70s style rock 'n' roll T-shirts, I gave up and reached for *Marie Claire.* The magazine fell open to a very interesting article indeed—"Sexual Secrets You Are Entitled to Know."

As a volunteer member of the Celibate Sista Brigade (CSB), the last thing I needed to be reading was yet another article on how to be the perfect lover. If there's one thing I've learned through all this it's when you're not getting any, sex is every-damn-where. You can't pick up a women's magazine or go to an internet site without reading all about the mysteries of Kama Sutra; the Catholic girl's guide to aural sex (say it to make him spray it); or the diary of some naughty-but-nice nymphomaniac. This at the same time my unused coochie was drying up and withering away like a pathetic little raisin in the sun.

Granted, wearing this illusory chastity belt was voluntary, and while I'd pleasantly surprised myself by my show of inner strength and self-regard, that didn't make my carnal urges any easier to endure. I'd had plenty of offers to end my drought since my breakup with Rodney—many by the man himself— but none that interested me. It's not hard to get laid if that's all you're looking for. In fact, with Rodney, and most men before him, that's all I got. For years I rode the baloney pony, knocked boots, hit the skins, got boinked, fucked, and screwed—did everything with many fine-ass-well-hung-tongue-of-life-but-couldn't-commit brothers *but* make love. It took me years to realize that in most cases I was addicted to the dick, not the man.

Now I wanted to experience sex in a loving, committed relationship. I was holding out for L.O.V.E. Though I have to be honest—after twenty-eight months (that's 852 days *without* a man's touch), lust was kicking my behind. I know there are charity fucks and auld lang syne fucks, but was there such a thing as a medicinal fuck? If there wasn't already, there should be, and believe me, I needed my prescription filled like a Westchester County socialite down to her last Prozac.

Giving in to my masochistic tendencies, I read on. I skimmed through the art of giving a hand job (apparently the most important part is the "twist over the top"); moved on to the importance of stimulating your man's testicles (sucking is good; biting is bad); and got to the part of adding fine jewelry to your sexual toy chest (who knew that pearls give the "perfect tickling sensation when draped around his penis and played with") before recognizing the familiar pull and tug of a turned-on clitoris. Immediately I slapped the cover closed and tossed the magazine aside.

The thought of pearls soaked in poontang juices and dangling around some beautiful, brown, rock-hard shaft was fueling my imagination and unmercifully teasing my body. I needed to get out of the bed, get to work, and take my mind off all things sexual.

"Make love not lust." I repeated my slogan, forcing myself to get up and head toward the bathroom. After a quick shower I threw on my work clothes—a layer of coconut-smelling sunblock and a slamming turquoise bikini. Before pulling on my skirt I took a quick look-see in the mirror, morphing into my best Tyra Banks swimsuit pose, complete with smoldering eyes and seductive pout.

"Pia Jamison, girl, you still got it going on," I congratulated myself. The glorious blue color played well against my mocha glazed skin. My breasts, pushed together by the strategically placed string tie between them, overflowed with tempting cleavage—just enough to be seductive, not enough to be raunchy. The scoop bottom sat below my navel, exposing my tiny dragon tattoo. I liked the way the high cut on my hips elongated my shapely legs and cupped my booty with a healthy heaping of Lycra love. The bathing suit cost me nearly $150, but it was worth it. I felt sexy and desirable. That's another thing I learned about celibacy. Even if you aren't givin' it up, it's important to look like you still might. You have to continue to feel attractive because the last thing you want is to be sitting at the singles bar of life sipping a no-sex cocktail with a low-self-esteem chaser.

I finished dressing and picked up my straw tote, packed with a Polaroid camera, film, sketch pad, a bottle of water, and my Hawaiian Tropic. I decided to throw in my Sony Discman with my favorite Will Downing CD, *Invitation Only,* then popped on my sunglasses and headed out the door. This was my last location check and the rest of the crew wasn't scheduled to arrive until tomorrow afternoon. I was anxious to finish up my phone calls and paperwork so I could grab a little "me" time before all hell broke loose on the work front. Apparently, I was going to need it. I had yet to meet or speak to the video's director, Grand Nelson, as he was a last-minute replacement. It seems that Keisha's manager (aka her mother) fell out with the original hire and demanded a new director for her little girl's new video. Word on the production grapevine was that Grand's résumé reel was an exercise in less-is-more. At this point he'd directed only two videos, but as Babyface Edmond's protégé, they were for none other than superstars Toni Braxton and TLC. Grand Nelson was now a hot commodity, but just in case he was also a raving lunatic, I planned to feel as stress-free as possible before the shoot began.

By the time the cab dropped me at Krell House, a private property that SunFire Productions had rented for the shoot, it was a little before eleven. With an awesome view of the Caribbean Sea and an isolated stretch of private beach, this incredible villa was an outstanding location. The owners were away and the beach was empty so I took a moment to witness the splendor of nature without the rude insertion of man. The color play of pale blue sky against sparkling aquamarine water and silky white sand was breathtaking. The bounce of the sunlight off the sea was perfect, as was the nearby cluster of graceful divi-divi trees standing like sculptures shaped by the breath of the island's refreshing trade winds. The Aruba Tourist Center boasted year-round sunshine, so hopefully conditions would be just as wonderful for the actual shoot. I took Polaroids from several angles so that Grand would have various options to work with when he arrived on Thursday to block the final shots. Wanting to be as thorough as possible, I also took the time to sketch out several ideas that were in the spirit of the storyboards but took in the realities of this landscape.

My work completed, I decided to mosey up the beach and take advantage of the solitude with a bit of topless sunbathing. I found a secluded niche tucked away in the rocks and claimed it as my own.

"Now *this* is the life," I whispered into the breeze as I disrobed down to my swimsuit bottoms and removed the beach essentials from my bag. I pushed my sunglasses onto the top of my head and applied a second coat of Hawaiian Tropic to my exposed shoulders, chest, and stomach. With Will Downing's sexy voice singing "If She Knew" in my ear, I stretched out into the warm sand and let the sun toast my nearly bare body. The combination of slippery oil on hot naked skin mixed with Will's lusty baritone voice let those pesky horn dogs loose, and released the sexy NC-17 movie stowed in my head.

From the central casting office in my mind emerged an impeccable male specimen zealous and eager to service my every physical need. His name was unknown, but his face and body were quite familiar to me. He was a sexy musician and my passionate costar, and within seconds I was transported onto the set of my long-running erotic fantasy.

It is late by the time I arrive at the club. The crowd has thinned considerably and only a few diehards—those unwilling to relinquish the night to sleep—remain.

I walk into the room, feeling quite horny, all in anticipation of being near him. The band is playing a jazzy version of Jon Lucien's "Sweet Control" and the seductive pull of the music heightens my desire. I pause before taking my seat to enjoy the splendor of him in his element. I watch closely, mesmerized by his presence. Everything about him reeks sensuality. The way he and his bass stand together like a loving couple, his arms draped possessively around her womanly curves. The way he gently holds the instrument upright, stroking her long slender neck with reverence and love—pulling from her belly the exact sound he desires and demands. The way his foot keeps perfect time to the music, gently twisting and turning his leg in and out, causing his tight thigh muscle to flex seductively through his trousers. The way his face contorts with both happiness and pain, giving the impression of orgasmic pleasure as the music consumes him. The sights and sounds of him continue to add layers to my desire and I feel my breasts begin to swell and my nipples grow longer as they strain against my dress in search of his mouth.

I take my seat in a darkened corner, where I have an unobstructed view of him. I close my eyes and let the music caress my body. It breezes over my skin like a sexy whisper, making my skin tingle and my clitoris engorge. I want to see the object of my desire. My eyes are drawn to the erect tip of his tongue penetrating the corner of his full lips. I watch him, lost in his performance, but can no longer hear. My brain is consumed with the image of him licking my clit with his incredibly talented tongue. I am getting so hot the faucets of my pussy are opening up and I can feel my juices begin to flow. I cross my legs and slowly clench the muscles of my vagina tight, enjoying the shift of pressure on my clit. As I continue to imagine him eating me, I can feel the wetness pooling in my panties. For an instant I wonder if anyone else can smell the scent of sex as it rises from my seat. My question is answered as the aroma seemingly wafts under his nose. He looks in my eyes and the intensity of his gaze, even for those few seconds, makes me melt.

I can no longer stand the absence of his touch. My pussy is about to explode. In search of relief, I slip my hand under the table and begin to finger myself through the thin silk of my dress. I close my eyes again as I masturbate, feeling my clit grow deliciously tighter and tighter. I open my eyes to make sure I am not being watched. I glance around the room. It is nearly deserted and those remaining have not noticed me. The band is playing a new song now, but I don't know what it is. I am too wrapped up in the thought of being wrapped up in him. Unconsciously I push my pelvis forward in search of his dick. I want to feel him inside me. I pull my panties to the side and begin to fuck myself with two fingers. The thought of him penetrating me, gliding in and out of my wet pussy, is driving me wild. I must keep myself from squirming too much in my seat as I get closer and closer to orgasm. I am glad the music is loud enough to mask the soft groans that escape my mouth. Oh shit, I'm coming. The contractions around my fingers are so powerful—I can only hope that I look like I'm enjoying the music and nothing more. I open my eyes to find him watching me. He subtly wets his lips and moves his bass slightly to the side. I can see the outline of his erection through his pants. As our eyes lock in an arousing gaze, I lift my hand from between my legs and gently lick the remaining juices from my drenched fingers...

Off in the distance, the sound of an appreciative voice saying "Oh, shit" interrupted my fantasy and forced my eyes open. I quickly sat up and glanced around, but as far as I could see, the beach was still empty. Convinced I had simply heard my own thoughts, I stretched my body from fingers to feet, savoring the delicious sensations as my heartbeat and breath returned to normal. If I smoked, I would have lit up a cigarette; instead I opted for a quick nap.

When I awoke, feeling refreshed and momentarily satisfied, it was after three o'clock. I quickly got dressed, packed my bag, and decided to walk the mile or so from the villa back to the Marriott. The afternoon sun was bright and strong. I reached for my sunglasses only to find them missing. I stopped and rummaged through my tote, but still came up empty-handed. Damn—that was the second pair I'd lost in six months.

By the time I got back to my room I was starving and still horny. Sex-lite will do that to you. It's like being on a low-carbohydrate diet and eating a bagel. You scoop out the good, doughy part and eat the crusty shell. While your stomach thinks it's getting bread, your palate is only partially fulfilled. The vagina, just like the mouth, knows the difference between gourmet sex and the diet plate.

I finished documenting the Polaroids and jotted down more notes before taking my second shower of the day. I slid into a slinky orange sundress and a pair of silver high-heel sandals. After adding a generous spritz of my favorite Issey Miyake cologne, I headed downstairs to the hotel restaurant for an early dinner.

I approached the gentleman at the podium and requested a table for one. I followed him through the restaurant, happily acknowledging the appreciative eyes turning in my direction.

As I passed his table, one particularly fine brother with a bald head laid a smile on me that could only be described as sunshine personified. I grinned back, making friendly eye contact, but kept on walking when I noticed a woman's handbag next to the plate across from him.

Sitting two tables away was another hot-looking brother, wearing dreadlocks and funky square black frames, eating alone while deeply engrossed in the latest Easy Rawlins adventure. As I passed him my perfume must have tapped him on the shoulder because out of the corner of my eye I noticed his attention turn from his moving tale to mine.

Go Pia, go Pia I sang silently, enjoying the mini whirl of attention. The host led me to a small table on the perimeter of the room. He pulled the table out as I slid gracefully onto the upholstered bench. Before departing, he handed me a menu and introduced me to my waiter, Duane. Duane took my drink order and left me to peruse the menu. Feeling eyes on me, I looked up and saw an attractive white gentleman smiling in my direction. I smiled back and he raised his wineglass in a silent toast. Apparently my mojo was in overdrive.

Duane returned shortly with my Cosmopolitan and a glass of champagne.

"I didn't order this," I informed him, pointing to the flute.

"A gentleman asked that this be sent to you with his compliments."

"Which gentleman?"

"I'm sorry, miss. I don't know. His instructions were left at the host station, along with this," he said, handing me a folded cocktail napkin addressed to "The Beautiful Lady in Orange."

I looked past the white man and saw that both brothers were gone, though the woman with the handbag at the bald man's table was back, sipping her coffee. "Thanks," I said, taking the note. I quickly placed my dinner order and following Duane's departure, unfolded the napkin.

Good evening, Beautiful Lady,

First, I must say that you really are a very sensuous woman. I truly enjoyed being with you today, even though you didn't know I was there. After seeing you on the beach, I've had nothing but erotic thoughts of you. I'm living in a dream world this afternoon full of fantasies of you and me and the things that we could do together.

Fantasy lovers can be so stimulating. Don't you agree? If the idea of a sexy mind-job appeals to you, and you're interested in a little anonymous pleasure by phone, call me this evening in room 420. I will be waiting patiently to hear your voice and tell you how I made love to you today. Don't be frightened, beautiful lady, I only want to whisper naughty things in your ear. I want you as wet as I am hard.

I refolded the napkin and resisted the urge to mop my hot and embarrassed face with it. The humiliation of being caught masturbating by a complete stranger caused me to down the champagne in one desperate gulp. I chased the bubbles down with a healthy swig of my vodka cocktail. By the time Duane returned with my dinner I had lost my appetite but had gained a nice little buzz—and the realization that while getting caught with my pants down was indeed humiliating, it felt hell of sexy too.

They say words beg for reality. Well, I am here to tell you that no truer statement has ever been made. As I strolled through the lobby trying to hide my flushed and flustered state behind a calm and confident stride, I could feel my embarrassment dissipate. Rising up in its place was a defiant cry from a unified body demanding immediate sexual gratification.

I pushed the button to call the elevator, praying that it would be empty for my ride up to the tenth floor. Gratefully alone in the lift, I again unfolded the napkin and reread the deliciously disturbing words, concentrating on the line "if you're interested in a little anonymous pleasure by phone, call me."

Pleasure by phone? Who did he think I was, Girl Six? Some cheap dial-a-ho? I thought in a lame attempt to temper my lust with outraged logic. *Why would I want to have phone sex with someone I've never laid eyes on?*

But he's had his eyes all over you and you love it, the little slut on my shoulder shouted. *Call him. You know you want to.*

According to the number he'd given me, Mr. Help Yourself to a Peek was a hotel guest. On a long shot, I called the operator and asked for the name of the person in room 420. But, just as I knew she would, she informed me that my request was against hotel policy.

Just call him, the voice inside demanded.

What if this guy is crazy or some sick degenerate? I already know that he's a voyeuristic peeping tom. A peeping tom who makes your panties wet.

True that, I concurred silently, as I headed to the minibar. I needed another strong dose of liquid courage because I was curious and horny—a combustible combination that left me no choice but to make that call.

Guzzling down my Finlandia vodka and tonic, I closed the drapes, turned off the lights, went straight to the bed, and sat down. I took a few seconds to listen to the waves crash on the beach and enjoy my fuzzy head before picking up the phone and dialing 0420. Before it rang, I hung up. *What the hell was I thinking?*

Before I came up with a reply my fingers began dialing again.

"Hello there," answered a deep and smoky voice. Those two simple words, spoken in a deep buttery timbre that was soothing and seductive, melted over my body and left me a drunk, horny, gooey mess. Suddenly, I could not wait for this man to wrap his words around my body.

"I got your note," I said softly.

"I'm glad you called."

"Do I know you? Have we met?"

"We've never met, but somehow it feels as if we're already lovers."

I guess you just delve right in, I thought, wondering if there were any rules to the phone-sex game. The only one that mattered to me was that we remained completely anonymous.

"Yes, I guess you would," I admitted, embarrassment tingeing my voice.

"Please don't be embarrassed. Women like you turn me on."

"Women like what?"

"Sensual, independent, strong women."

"And how can you tell so much about me?" I asked, intrigued that he had, even if he was only bullshitting, read me pretty damn accurately.

"Actions do speak louder than words," the amazing voice informed me. "It's obvious that you're a woman who's aware of her body and knows what she likes. A woman who's not afraid to touch herself."

"You know, this is very unfair," I said coyly as I began to get my flirt on. "You've seen me in one of my, shall we say, most intimate moments. You know how I look, but I know nothing about you. Like what's your name?"

"Call me whatever you'd like. I am whoever you want me to be. I look the way you want me to look, dress the way you want me to dress, live the way you want me to live. I'm the perfect man—your dream lover, your ultimate partner."

"Okay, fair enough. I'll call you Fin," I announced, eyeing the empty vodka bottles on the bed. "But you must tell me something about yourself. What are some of your favorite things?"

"My favorite things...let's see... Kissing is definitely on the top of my list. I love to play with lips, teeth, and tongue. And I'm also very fond of giving tongue massages," the sexy voice revealed.

Oh shit, I thought. This man...his voice...I was definitely intrigued, undeniably hot, and getting more and more comfortable with the idea of mind-fucking this erotic stranger.

"And I am quite capable of putting my tongue anywhere."

"Anywhere?" I asked, the Finlandia making me bold.

"Anywhere, baby. Is that what you'd like? For me to give you a tongue bath? For me to put my tongue in places you always wanted one to go and in some you thought it shouldn't?"

"Yes," I agreed and begged at the same time. I swear I could feel his warm breath coming through the phone and fondling my ears and neck.

"Well, then you're going to have to take off your panties. Will you do that for me?"

"Yes," I said, my voice dropping to a faint hush. I cradled the phone between my shoulder and ear and slid off my thong. I also slipped out of my dress and stretched out on the bed, cradling the receiver to my face like a lover's hand.

"Are they off?"

"Yes, everything is."

"Ooh. Now that's a beautiful visual. Just thinking about you naked is getting me so aroused. If you could see me now, you'd know just how much."

"I can see."

"I'm there with you?"

"Yes. You're here and I can feel your hands on my body. They're soft and strong."

"How am I touching you?" he asked.

"With light, feathery caresses," I whispered as I spread my legs open.

"I want to play with your magnificent breasts and feel your nipples as hard as my dick is right now. Would you like that?"

"Yes."

This stranger's voice was seductive and hypnotic and I felt myself slipping into a deep sensual stupor. He was filling my head with erotic reveries and by the power of suggestion I found myself touching my breasts. I bit my lower lip as my hands became his, stroking my thighs, belly, arms, and breasts, pinching and rolling my stiff nipples between his fingers.

"You have an amazing body. I am so hard now that I have to loosen my pants so I can breathe."

"Then take them off," I suggested. I hung on while he removed his clothes, trying to imagine what he looked like. If his voice was any indication, the boy was fine.

"Oh yes, that's much better. Now I can feel the smooth length of your body pressed up against mine," he said.

"I can feel you too. You're very hard."

"All for you, baby. I'm sucking on your nipples and licking the valley between your breasts until it's wet and shiny. Now I'm rubbing myself between them. Do you like that?"

"Yes," I replied as my hand slipped down between my thighs.

"Tell me what you feel."

"Hmm. I feel your shaft sliding between my breasts. I'm squeezing them closer so I can feel every ridge of your penis as it moves up and down my chest."

"Should I move fast or slow?"

"Slow, Fin. Move real slow so I can catch you in my mouth. Can you feel me flicking my tongue around your tip?" I asked, amazed by how much I was getting into this.

"I can feel it, baby, and it feels good," Fin replied, his breath getting slower and his voice huskier. It was obvious that he was just as turned on by our encounter as I was. His desire was fueling my bravado.

"Hmm, you're so hard, Fin. My pussy is getting so wet and juicy just thinking about it," I told him as I massaged the fleshy mound of my pubis with slow, languid circular motions.

"I know, baby. I can smell you. Your love smells sweet and briny, just like seawater and sunshine. My mouth is watering for your beautiful pussy."

"Hmm. Would you like to taste me?" I asked, feeling the torturous ecstasy of an engorged clitoris.

"Yes, I want to eat you."

"And I want you too—but first I want to take you in my mouth. Can you feel the wet warmth surround your shaft as I suck you?"

"Ooh. God, yes. Yeah, baby. My dick is like a rod moving between your soft, cushiony lips."

"What should I do now?" I ask, sending slight smacking and sucking noises though the phone.

"Play with my balls."

"I'm licking them now. Does that feel good, or would you rather I suck them?"

"Tickle them with your hair and suck my dick," he moaned.

"Fast or slow?"

"Fast *and* slow. Tease me, baby. Make me crazy like you did this afternoon."

"I'm sucking you fast right now. My head is hanging over your lap and my hair is brushing your belly. I can feel you get longer and harder in my mouth."

"Mmm..."

"Now I'm slowly running my tongue around the ridge at the head of your dick. Do you like that?" I asked, feeling breathlessly brazen.

I could hear him masturbating. His soft moans and gentle grunts were an indication of his approaching orgasm. His desire was making me so hot and I wanted to feel him inside me. I parted my labia and gently penetrated the soft fleshy pulp of my vagina with my fingers.

"Fin?"

"Yes, baby."

"Do me."

"How?"

"Put my legs on your shoulders. I want you deep inside me."

"Oh yes, baby. I love the way your golden brown skin looks against mine."

"Move it slow and gentle. In and out, in and out...ooh."

"You are so hot and wet. My dick is just sloshing through all of your glorious pussy juice."

"Now harder and faster," I commanded, my fingers reacting to the sound of my voice as my pelvis rose and fell against my hand.

"You are so beautiful, baby. Seeing you...on the beach...fucking yourself...Oh, girl you turn me on so much. I want to come for you."

His words, sweet and lusty, fondled the very core of my pleasure zone. In my mind I could see my legs on his shoulders as he pumped me. That vision sent me over the edge and I felt myself on the verge of coming.

"I want you to come all over my breasts. Come for me, Fin."

"Shit...Oh yeah...ah...ah...ah," he screamed into my ear as he reached his orgasm. I could hear him breathing hard as his body recovered from his climax.

His pleasure released mine and I followed him with one of the most intense, head-banging orgasms I've ever experienced. I announced my climax with a series of sweet groans followed by one long, stress-busting exhale while my vagina throbbed with potent, delicious contractions. As I luxuriated in the aftermath of coming, I kept thinking that even while I had managed to maintain my celibacy and explore a new and exciting avenue of sexual expression, I had just experienced the most mind-blowing physical gratification with a man I didn't know and would never see.Either I was hell of adventurous or incredibly pathetic. Nonetheless, I felt totally satiated and that's all that really mattered at this point.

I could hear Fin snoring lightly through the receiver. *I guess even the perfect man falls right to sleep after sex,* I laughed to myself. I softly said goodnight and, receiving no reply, hung up the phone. Before turning in myself, I called to request an 8:30 wake-up call, instinctively knowing that after such a powerful sexual experience I was going to need help getting up in time for the morning's production meeting.

The phone rang right on time, waking me from the most restful night of sleep I'd had since arriving in Aruba. As the cobwebs cleared from my head, they were replaced by momentary confusion. Did last night really happen or did I simply experience an extremely erotic, alcohol-induced dream? I sat up and looked around the room for confirmation. There beside me on the bed lay my touch-tone lover, right where I left it after last night's encounter. My panties and dress were strewn at the foot of the bed, along with the empty miniature bottles of Finlandia. I took a minute to smile and bask in the memory of last night before jumping out of bed to get ready for work.

Showered and dressed in black Capri pants and a backless T-shirt, I strolled into the conference room. Most of the crew had already arrived and were snacking on bagels and Danish while waiting for the director to arrive. I walked over to the silver urn and poured myself a cup of coffee. Just as I reached for the Equal, I heard a familiar voice that made my breathing cease and my groin tingle.

"Good morning. I hope you slept well," he said. I slowly turned around and looked into the face of the bald brother with the sunshine smile from the restaurant. Embarrassment plucked the words from my mouth and carried them away like crows pilfering a cornfield. I stood there mute and mortified.

"I believe these belong to you," he said, handing me my lost sunglasses.

"Thank you," I managed to say. He smiled again and walked to the front of the room to begin the meeting. I went in the opposite direction, taking a seat at the far end of the table.

"I'm Grand Nelson and we'll all be spending a lot of time together these next few days." He bombarded me with a deadly grin that started in his warm, sexy eyes and gently pulled at the corners of his lips before erupting into an all-knowing, I've-got-a-secret smile.

All I could do was bite my lower lip in anticipation and make sure my hands were on the table in full view.

The Spice Woman
Ethel Mack-Ballard

Prologue

You may well ask who I am, for I see you do not recognize me. But deep in the far reaches of your mind you have heard my voice. I am a teller of tales, a spinner of magic and fantasy. And tonight I have come to spin for you a story of eroticism and mystery. Give me your undivided attention and let me slip into your mind as gently as fog steals from the ocean's breast. Close your eyes and visualize the scenes I describe to you for it will be as if you are the one of whom I speak, as if these are your thoughts, your touch, your fears, and your ecstasy. Now, if you are ready, I will relate to you the story of the Spice Woman.

• • •

A man weary beyond his years, weary to the depths of his soul, has sought refuge in a rented Victorian overlooking the ocean. The house is situated on a small bluff rising above the Monterey coastline. Surrounded by brush and stubble, it fades into the natural landscape. Its buff-colored paint is peeling and the steps to the veranda sag. A steep incline leads to the beach below. The area is isolated, about a mile from the main road. The nearest neighbor shelters in a house of redwood and glass which can be seen around the curve of the beach on a rocky bluff several miles away.

This man is a refugee from the civilized frenzy of the city. In this furnished house, which he has taken for one month, he has found a haven, a resting-place. He loves the high-ceilinged rooms, the bare wood floors, and the ornate carved banister bordering the staircase, the floor-length stained glass window on the landing spilling jeweled messages into the entry hall below. The kitchen is stocked and he has provided himself with a small wine cellar and several bottles of good cognac that he sips from a heavy lead-crystal glass before the fireplace in the parlor as he listens to the ocean's evening song. There is no telephone. He wants no communication with the outside world. He hears only the sound of the wind sighing around the corners of the house, the rhythmic lapping of waves breaking against the shore. He thinks he is at peace. He thinks he has brought to heel those emotions that in the past have pained him so.

He spends his days puttering about the neglected herb garden discovered behind the house or walking along the beach in the early morning mist. In the evening he sits on the veranda watching the sun surrender its golden flames to the onslaught of twilight and he dreams of a woman—a woman he sees only in his mind's eye. Her features are blurred yet he knows her, recognizes in her some hidden remembrance of passion that he has smothered in himself.

His days are even and uneventful, but his nights are spent in troubled dreams barely remembered in the pearl light of dawn. Dreams that cause him to soil the sheets or to awaken suddenly with an erection so powerful that the pain is a sweet ecstasy. Sometimes he thinks he hears someone calling him, sighing his name as if the sound were carried on a breeze. It seems to come from the attic, but when he explores (in the bright glare of daylight) there is only the usual clutter one finds in such places—boxes, trunks, broken toys, and an old brass bed with a bare mattress partially covered by a hand-crocheted bedspread. Light filters through dusty dormer windows and cobwebs gleam in the rafters and in the corners.

One night during the second week of his residence in the old house, he is awakened by a voice heard only in his thoughts. As if in a trance, he leaves his bed and walks down the darkened hall to the attic stairs. His naked skin pimples in the chill air and his bare feet make light slapping sounds as he mounts the steps. When he opens the door, he is encompassed by a halo of light. The moon is so bright the entire room is illuminated in a silvery glow. When he crosses the threshold he feels a little dizzy and slightly disoriented. It takes a moment to right himself. Then, to his amazement, he sees the familiar attic is transformed. Lace curtains covering the open windows blow gently in the breeze. In the light, cobwebs sparkle as if woven of iridescent silk, and the brass bed is sheeted and draped with material that has the sheen of satin.

He moves closer to the bed. A woman lies shadowed against the pale sheets. The room is filled with her scent. She smells of nutmeg, cinnamon, and the faintest suggestion of almonds. She is covered with a diaphanous veil. Her naked body, the color of rosewood, shines as if oiled. She lies sprawled like a rag doll tossed carelessly upon the bed. One leg slightly raised, the other at an angle. Her thighs are parted. Her left arm lies across her bosom and her thumb gently caresses the pouting nipple of her right breast, outlined by the thin veil. Her right hand rests between her legs. She is slowly stroking her sex through the protective cover of the translucent material. Her head is turned toward him. Her dark hair is a woolen crown of ebony. Her eyes are open but slightly slit as she awards him the brief white flash of her smile. She sighs, and slowly lifts the veil until it forms a scarf around her throat.

Her body lies exposed and vulnerable. She welcomes his gaze. He moves closer and his nostrils widen as the musk of her woman-scent floats toward him. She strokes her belly, that soft round mound dimpled by her navel, and lowers her hand to the tip of her budding clitoris, which he can barely see. She teases it, dusting her fingertips across it like a feather, then slides the palm of her hand over her mound and shakes it gently, slipping her fingers in the opening from which the honeyed juice begins to spill. "Oh..." she sighs. "Oh..." And her hips dance against the pale bedsheets.

As he watches this woman make love to herself, his body flushes with heat. His penis is engorged and pulsing with blood. She has turned her head toward the window and, unconcerned that he is watching, brings herself to a moaning climax. Her buttocks tighten, her hips churn, and her back arches. Suddenly she collapses and lies limp, panting, twisting on the bed. She murmurs his name without moving her lips, calling him with her mind. He lowers himself onto the bed and places his hands over hers at the entrance to her sex. She slides her hand back and inserts his fingers into the hot, moist recesses of that second mouth all women possess, then withdraws them dewed with her fluids, perfumed with her juices.

She seeks him with her hand, fingers teasing, dancing, grasping. His penis is hard and smooth and she seems pleasured by the look of it, the taste of it, as she leans forward and flicks her tongue over the head. He tastes of salt, sweat, and smoky wine. She pulls him into her mouth so greedy with desire that he wants to spill himself into that warm receptacle, but she will not allow this. Releasing him, she guides him over her. Her thighs are soft but strong. They encircle his waist as he enters her smoothly, firmly. She is like a furnace! Her heat engulfs him. He slides his hands beneath her hips, raising her closer to him, and with each thrust he can feel her muscles pull at him, sucking him deeper into herself. The crinkling hairs of her mound cling to those surrounding his groin. A fine mist of sweat covers their bellies. His hands are filled with her breasts; her body is saturated with the moisture of lovemaking.

She moans under him and moves in invitation to be taken even more fiercely. He leans back on his heels, pulling her into a seated position on his lap. She flings her arms about his neck. He circles her waist and draws her tightly against him. She is like a fever! Everywhere his skin touches her, he burns. Her fingers are flames dancing through his hair, across his chest. With her weight she pushes him backward until she is astride him and he has entered her so deeply he has touched the wall of her womb.

She bucks above him, head thrown back, eyes closed, palms pushing against his shoulders. She is a shadow woman writhing in the moonlight. Her spice scent floods the room and underneath, the hot pungent smell of sex. He feels himself swelling even more, rising to her body's silent commands. He grinds into her, exploding in tiny volcanic eruptions until finally, as her mind screams his name, he releases a gushing fountain, a roaring river. Her skin glows copper-red in the heat of her coming. She is all the colors of the stained glass window on the staircase landing, rainbowed in her ecstasy. He gasps with the power of his climax and brings her down to him, burying his face in the cushion of her breasts, then seeks the hollow of her throat to suck the tiny pulsing vein through which the blood races so swiftly, sings so sweetly. His lips, his tongue, his mouth devour hers. Spent, she is limp against him, surrendering completely to his dominance. For these few brief moments she is his and his alone. She folds herself beside him and sighs deep in her throat. The sigh becomes a purr and he imagines a sleek mountain lioness warming him through the night.

When he awakes, the morning light streaming from the dormer windows causes him to blink. He rolls over and discovers that he is lying naked on the dusty bare mattress of the old brass bed. The crocheted coverlet lies crumpled on the floor. No lace curtains swing in the breeze. The magic is gone and he is lost and bewildered in the sun's bright rays.

For several days he wanders about the house talking aloud, lecturing himself, convincing himself that what he experienced was merely a vivid dream. But each time he ventures near the attic stairs, his nostrils flare as he picks up the woman's musk whispering beneath the scent of spice.

He becomes despondent and lies on his bed in the dark trying to coax with his hands the exquisite orgasm that had consumed him that night. Was his desire and fulfillment only an illusion? He thinks not, for in the midnight hours he still hears the faint echo of her calling. The persistence of that mind-voice beckons him, but when he rushes to the attic he finds it empty and untouched by the sexual substance of his dreams.

Days pass and one night during an electrical storm when the elements threaten to rip the roof from the house, boil the waters of the ocean, and scatter sand from the beach out into the atmosphere, he hears her call. His mind floods with the force of his desire. He approaches the passage to the attic slowly, clutching an old woolen robe about his naked body. When he reaches the door he hesitates, wondering if he might be on the brink of insanity. But the power of her summons forces him forward. It is as he remembered. The attic gleams in the moonlight. Lace curtains stir in the breeze at the open windows. The brass bed is dressed in white satin shimmering in the silvery glow. No woman reclines on the bed but spice infuses the air. He knows she is nearby. He can sense the pulse of her blood, the beat of her warm heart. He turns and sees her moving toward him as if floating. Her scent precedes her. The diaphanous gown caresses the curves of her body. Her eyes are gold and black, diamond-pointed like a cat's. Her head is held proudly and her silky brown skin begins to glow

as she moves toward him. Her spice intoxicates him; he is
drunk with the essence of her. Gently, she takes him by the
hand and crosses to the bed, where she seats him at the foot.
Lifting her hand, she gestures behind her. In the shadows, by a
wicker chair, he perceives another figure. It is a woman.

She steps into the pool of light spilling from a window. She
wears a hooded cape that swirls about her feet as she advances
toward the bed. The Spice Woman reaches for her sister and
they undress one another slowly. The Spice Woman's naked
body radiates shades of honey and gold, chocolate and ebony,
rosewood and caramel. The other astounds him for never has
he imagined a woman like this. Before his eyes is a true albino.
She is pale to the point of translucence. Her hair is silver-
white, her eyes pink-white, her body full-breasted. Blue veins
pulse beneath the vitreous skin. She is so white, so pale that
even moonlight cannot gift her skin. Her pubic hair shines sil-
vered and here and there specks of glitter costume the nest of
her sex. She stretches herself upon the bed. Her limbs are long
and elegant and her body emanates an air of coldness. He
thinks of icebergs, mysterious and majestic, floating in the
Arctic Sea. The nipples of her breasts are milk white, the aure-
ole only slightly darker than heavy cream. She moves
languorously, as if any effort is too much for her to bear. The
two bodies, one pale but lit with a soft glow as if it were the
most precious of pearls, and the other awash with color, limbs
of topaz and molten copper, mesmerize the man.

The women turn to one another and begin to make love.
They are like mirror twins. One touches a breast; the other
strokes the nipple. One slips her fingers into all the secret
places, chased by the other's fingers, hands, lips. The man has
never seen two women together and at first he feels like an
intruder. But their sighs and moans stir him and he becomes
aroused. He leans toward them. The Albino smiles without
showing her teeth. Her eyelids are pink-glowing. She lifts a

languid hand and beckons to him. Throwing off his robe, he crawls beside her and she takes his hand and places it at the base of her throat. Her skin is cold, but it burns as ice burns, as the Spice Woman's skin burns like fire. Each woman can consume him in her own way.

He places his lips on the Albino's throat; the pulse is slow and faint. He seeks her mouth. Her tongue is cool, receptive. She invites him to cover her and he lies down upon her, sinking into the soft resilience of her body. Her hair sparkles with glitter, as does the fine down under her arms. He sees the Spice Woman lying open-legged, her body gleaming with the heat of her passion, caressing herself as the Albino draws him into her embrace.

Her arms are chill winds, her breasts pointed icicles, her mouth a cold cave lit by a distant fire, and he is ensnared by her erotic aloofness. When he slides into her it is as if he has waded into an icy mountain stream. Her chilly arms enfold him, her cool breath sighs against his cheek. She caresses his back, his buttocks, nips the vulnerable artery at the base of this throat. He strokes within her, thrusting without releasing his full strength while she moves against him slowly.

Her passion does not boil as that of the Spice Woman. It builds almost without his knowledge until suddenly he is gasping and ready for release. She pinches gently at the root of his stem holding him in check as the Spice Woman lies on top of him. Together they turn and he is caught between summer and winter, fire and ice. The women caress and stroke him until his skin comes alive. They lick the hairs on his arms and chest. They part his thighs and wash the hair surrounding his genitals with their tongues. His penis awakens more fully, fused with blood, hot and pulsing.

They alternate taking the first drops of male wine that seep from the head. Their fingers and hands choreograph dances along his spine and across his belly, they compose concertos along the length of his arms and legs. They tease and fondle him until their fingers are covered with his scent. He is wild with passion, loving the icy reserve of one, the fiery abandonment of the other.

When he takes the Albino, his thrusts are timed and patterned like some ancient court dance. When he takes the Spice Woman, he improvises moves he had never thought possible. Each woman writhes beneath him, atop him, beside him. He takes them in every way. He feasts on the cool or heat of their breasts, caressing the soft mounds of their buttocks. He rejoices in the chill wine or hot brandy taste of their second mouths as he slips his tongue along the flowers that open only for him. He tastes the nectar that flows only for him.

He is delirious with the texture of their skin, the sound of their mind-voices, the pure eroticism of their lovemaking. When he is ready for release, they will not allow him to choose between them. Instead they force him to lie with one on each side. As one encloses his throbbing penis in her hand, the other gently cradles the sac below while they entice him to give up his wine into their mouths without knowing which is which.

During the night he is lulled by the smell of the Spice Woman and the faint lilac odor of the Albino. They fold their limbs around him, draw the coverlet about their shoulders, whispering him to sleep with the songs of their minds. He drifts, rocked in the arms of his shadow lovers.

When he wakes, the sun is setting. He watches the orange-gold rays descend into the west as if the sun were lowering itself to bathe in the warm waters of the Pacific Ocean. He listens to the music of the waves and sniffs the air for the scent of his ghost women. Surely they could not have been real. But scattered across the surface of the dusty mattress he sees specks of silver and gold glitter. The air smells of a mixture of lilac and spice.

The next day the man contacts the agent who arranged for his rental of the old Victorian. He leases the house for a year.

Homecumming
Cherysse Welcher-Calhoun

"Honey, I'm home," she announced dramatically to the empty house, kicking the door shut behind her. This was the first weekend in months that both of the kids would be away. "Of all the Fridays in the year," she said out loud, as though her husband were standing there listening, "you have to work overtime on this one." She walked through the living room, down the hall, and into their bedroom. She shed her coat, purse, newspaper, and the toys the kids had left in the backseat of her car. Then she rushed into the bathroom to pee. She'd known she had to go when she left work, but didn't want to waste even a moment of this precious weekend, so she held it until she made it home. If she'd worn stockings, she probably wouldn't have made it. "Thank God for dress-down Fridays," she said out loud as she relieved the pressure on her bladder.

The house was empty, quiet. She decided that she would take this rare opportunity to soak in the bathtub to pass the time until her husband returned home. She removed her faded blue jeans, royal blue panties, and socks all in one motion. From the toilet, she could see that she would have to clean the tub before using it. Her daughter's "Bath Time Elmo" lay at the bottom. She hadn't planned on cleaning the bathroom until tomorrow—after she and her husband had slept in, something they hadn't been able to do months. She thought perhaps she'd get up briefly and make them a nice breakfast, something with grits. He'd like that. Then they'd eat leisurely in bed and cuddle up for the rest of the morning.

She released a tired breath, wiped herself, and flushed. She picked up her clothing from the floor and dumped it into the hamper. She pulled the sweatshirt she was wearing over her head, catching her silver hoop earring. "Damn!" she winced as the heavy shirt pulled on her earlobe. She felt uncomfortable standing there with her shirt twisted over her head and no panties on. Out of habit, she went into the bedroom and closed the door. Usually, one of her kids, if not both, would be lurking in the shadows, waiting for her to try and be alone. She'd try to sneak into the bathroom for some quiet time. But it wouldn't be long before one of them knocked on the door to tattle on the other, ask for assistance with something, or just have a conversation about the day's events through the locked bathroom door. If she ignored them, they assumed she didn't hear them and would beat on the door until her husband made them stop. "You all right in there, Baby?" he'd say.

Once she extricated herself and her earring from the sweatshirt, she returned to the bathroom in her royal blue bra, the other half of the matching set that her husband had given her for her last birthday. She had been so pleased that he bought her something so sexy after all these years. She reached down into the cabinet under the sink for the Comet and a raggedy sponge. When she stood up, she caught her reflection in the mirror that ran the full length of the wall behind the sink. Her husband said she looked even better than when he'd first set eyes on her, as though she were the only one who could see the evidence of two pregnancies on her stomach and thighs. She leaned into the mirror and rubbed her fingertips over her tired face. Then she leaned back and looked at her breasts. Her nipples were pushing against the silky fabric of the bra, and she rubbed her fingers over them.

"Shit," she said, whispering out of habit so the kids wouldn't hear her swear. "It's cold in here." She frequently carried on a running dialogue with herself while she moved about the house picking up behind the kids and her husband, while she cooked or vacuumed or did laundry. But usually her voice just blended with the other sounds that made their house a home. The whirring and humming of the washer and dryer, the children and their friends running up and down the hall, laughing or yelling at each other, the tinkle and splash of dishes being done, the chopping and rattling of pots and pans as food was prepared, the music from the stereo establishing the underlying rhythm for the rest of the noise. And above it all would be the deep, booming voice of her husband, playing with the children, laughing with his friends, or having a one-way dispute with a referee on television who had just made a bad call against the home team. She loved the sound of his voice. She began unhooking her bra as she went out into the hallway to turn the heater up, then walked into the living room to put on some music.

Back in the bathroom, she bent over the side of the tub, trying not to inhale the fumes from the cleanser as Erica Badu's seductive voice swept through the house, filling the quiet spaces. She scrubbed all the essential places, making a personal promise to do a more thorough job the following day. She reached up for the shower massage and rinsed the pale green residue from the tub. Then she closed the drain and turned the knob to the right to run her bath water. She found the lavender bath gel her husband had bought for her at an expensive boutique in Carmel on the same birthday he'd given her the underwear.

She decided to make herself a drink while the tub filled, and went into the kitchen to see what was available. She was hoping for something that would give her a quick buzz without the headache. She found an almost-full bottle of dark rum she'd bought earlier that winter to make her husband hot toddies when he was down with the flu. There was vodka from the last football party, and her personal favorite, José Cuervo. She opened the refrigerator door to look for margarita mix, and the magnet holding her son's list of chores fell to the floor.

"Now that would be too much like right for anything I want to be in here," she said, realizing that they were out of mix. "Fuck it." She grabbed the bottle of tequila and a shot glass and headed back to the bathroom. She set the tall bottle and the short glass on the commode and dipped her fingers into the steaming water of the tub.

"Ow!" she cried, snatching her hand from the water. She laughed at her foolishness and turned the knob slightly to the left to cool the water. She unscrewed the cap on the tequila and poured herself a drink. Her husband had taught her the proper way to drink tequila on one of their first dates, but she hadn't felt like going through the trouble of slicing a lime or bringing the salt shaker to the bathroom just for herself. She tilted the glass to her lips and swallowed the contents in one gulp.

"Whew!" she said, shaking her head and shoulders. Her husband always said "the first one is the worst one." She screwed the top back on the tequila and noticed that there was cleanser under her nails. She used the fingernail brush to scrub her hands and dried them on her son's pajama bottoms, which hung from a hook on the back of the door. As she walked back into the bedroom to find her vanilla-scented candles, the phone rang.

"Hello?" she said.

"Hey, Baby." It was her husband. "What chu doin'?" he asked. She loved hearing his voice on the phone, and pressed the received closer to her ear.

"Nothing," she responded. "I was getting ready to take a bath. What's up with you?"

"Just wanted to see if you're enjoying your little moment alone," he said. "That's all."

"Oh," she said, disappointed. She was hoping he was calling to say that he was coming home early. "So, what time are you getting off?"

"Soon as I get home," he teased. It took her a second to realize what he meant.

"Shut up," she said, a broad smile spreading across her face. She stroked the skin between her breasts, where she could still feel the warmth of the tequila. Her nipples were erect again, but this time it wasn't because of the cold. The more she heard his voice, the more excited she became, and while he told her about the latest drama on the job she listened just to feel his voice resonate throughout her body. She held the phone between her chin and shoulder and slid her hands over her body, pretending they were his hands softly caressing her.

"So, what time are you coming home?" she interrupted.

"I'm supposed to be off at 1:00 A.M.," he replied, "but if it's slow I'll be able to leave early. You want me to bring you anything?"

"Just you."

"Okay, Baby," he said, recognizing the disappointment in her voice. "I'm gonna get home as soon as I can, all right?"

"Okay," she said softly. "I miss you."

"See you in a minute, Baby."

She returned to the bathroom. The tub was full and she turned off the water, then poured herself another shot. She lit two candles, flicked off the overhead light, and eased one foot into the bath water. It was still a little hot, but she figured it wouldn't take long to cool. She lowered herself into the water inch by inch, allowing her body to acclimate to the temperature.

Once she was seated in the tub, she breathed in the steamy air slowly and deeply, then exhaled as the water's warmth wrapped around her body. The light from the candle cast flickering shadows around the small room, and the sweet smell of vanilla lingered softly in the foggy air. She slid further down into the water so her chest was completely submerged. Her body relaxed, the day's tension melting away from her neck and shoulders. She closed her eyes, seduced by the music, the warmth of the water, and Mr. Cuervo. She awoke five minutes later, surprised that she'd fallen asleep so easily and so deeply.

When her eyes adjusted to the darkness, she reached for the bath gel and held it at arm's length above her, letting it pour out in a thin stream onto her stomach. She smoothed the gel across her belly and wrote her and her husband's names in the lather with her finger. She drew a big heart around their names and laughed at the memory of writing their initials in a sidewalk patch of wet cement back when they were courting. *Together forever,* he'd said. She poured more gel onto her washcloth and rubbed it over her body, shivering slightly at its coolness against her skin. She moved the towel in circles around her neck, down her back, over her shoulders and breasts. She raised one leg then the other and washed up to her toes.

Before she rinsed, she got up on her knees so that her vagina was just above the surface of the water. She added a little more gel to the washcloth and rubbed it between her legs and over her round behind. *Your ass is mine,* he often teased her. She smiled at the thought and began moving the cloth slowly back and forth between her legs. The cool air above her waist contrasted with the warm water around her hips and she arched her back to get the full effect of the sensation. She closed her eyes and began rotating her hips back and forth, pressing them into the hand that held the cloth.

"Can I join you?"

"Shit!" she shrieked, startled. Her husband stood naked in the bathroom doorway, holding two icy margaritas.

"I remembered we used the last of the mix and how much you like a good margarita," he said.

She was embarrassed—how long had he been standing there? "You scared the hell outta me!" She lowered her body back into the water and began to wash again as though that was all she'd been doing when he appeared. She dipped her cloth into the water and squeezed it out over her shoulders to rinse away the thick lather. She watched him walk towards her, his stiffening penis just about eye level. She was proud that she could still do that to him, pleased that he was watching her watch him.

"See something you like?" he asked with a cocky attitude, placing the margaritas on the sink.

"Oh, yeah," she blushed coyly, "I see a whole lot I like."

He reached down and cupped her breast under the water, then raised it above the surface, letting the water run off it. When she responded with a quiet moan, he gently pinched her nipple. Her body trembled as if suddenly chilled and his thick chocolate dick rose and jumped in reply. They both recognized the sound drifting through the doorway as the end of Erica Badu's last song on the CD. "I'll be right back," he said, standing up and walking toward the door.

"Damn!" she said. Her eyes were glued to his muscular back, firm behind, and strong thighs as he moved out of the room. "He is so fine." She thought of what possibilities the night held. She couldn't remember the last time they were able to make love without the kids around. Just think how adventurous they could get with the whole house to themselves.

By the time he returned she had rinsed herself off with the shower massage and was stepping out of the tub. "What took you so long?" she said as Luther Vandross's voice spilled into the room.

"I had to talk to Luther," he said, "and tell him what kind of sounds we wanted to hear tonight. He said he could handle it."

They both laughed. Her eyes followed her husband's hand to his dick and she was disappointed that he was now limp. She took it as a challenge—one she was definitely up to. She turned away from him and slowly and deliberately bent over the tub—much further than she needed to. She took her time turning on the faucet to replenish the hot water. Before she could straighten back up, he was behind her, his hands on her waist, pulling her hips onto his awakening penis. He pressed against her a little harder, bending his knees slightly to make sure he could slide along her pussy at just the right angle, but she stood and moved behind him, gently urging him towards the tub.

"Your turn," she said.

"Aw, Baby," he pleaded, reaching behind him to grab her. "I just wanna feel it."

"You will," she answered matter-of-factly. "Believe me, you will."

He stepped into the water without caution, then immediately sucked air through his teeth, making a hissing sound. "Damn, Baby," he said, trying not to let the water swish around his legs. "This shit is hot!"

"Stop cryin' and suck it up," she laughed, turning off the running water.

"Suck it up?" He looked at her like she was a crazy woman.

"Do unto others…" she said. He smiled back, showing his even white teeth and a glimpse of his thick pink tongue, then eased down into the water.

She pulled a clean washcloth from the towel rack and dunked it between his legs. She leaned behind him, letting her bare breasts brush across his skin, and squeezed water over his back. She repeated the action several times—until her nipples were hard again and he had become less sensitive to the heat. He leaned back against the tub and closed his eyes. She poured gel on the cloth and washed him gently while she surveyed his body. His skin was a milk-chocolate brown with red undertones. His bald head glistened with perspiration, his lips looked so full and soft, and his shoulders were smooth and strong. His body was a sculpted masterpiece, calling out to her fingertips, her mouth, her pussy.

She couldn't help touching him. She moved the washcloth over his body, making sure he stayed wet and warm all over. She ran it over his stomach and hipbones. His penis responded immediately, but she ignored it, teasing him by omission, and finished washing him down. She leaned forward, having saved his toes for last, and he sat up and kissed her softly up and down her spine. She closed her eyes, letting the sensation run between her legs.

"Ready to get out?" she asked.

He nodded yes, pulled himself to a standing position, and took the cloth from her. She watched as he washed himself in all the spots she couldn't reach, then rinsed the suds from his body with fresh water. When he turned off the spray, she began to lightly pat his body dry with a thick bath towel. He stepped out of the tub so that she could finish what she'd started. She knelt down in front of him to dry his calves and feet. He moved in closer to her. His penis was directly in front of her face, still only semi-erect.

"This simply will not do," she said. She dropped the towel at his feet and held his penis in her hands. He moaned. She brushed her moist lips against the smooth head of his penis. He moaned a little more. She reached behind her for the perfect margarita he'd made. She took a swallow then parted her lips and drew him into the wet, warm, salty haven of her mouth. He moaned louder this time.

"Mmph, mmph, mmph," he said from deep in this throat. He placed a hand on the back of her neck to let her know he was pleased. And she loved knowing that she was bringing him pleasure. She pulled his now fully erect dick slowly from her mouth, letting her lips drag over the head before sucking it back in. He flinched and she moved her tongue along his shaft. She knew his knees were getting weak because he grabbed hold of the towel rack to support himself. This excited her even more and she began to take him in and out with faster strokes. She could feel his dick expanding inside her mouth and knew he was nearing a point of no return. She slowly pulled him from between her lips and leaned away from him. She reached again for her drink and brought the glass to his penis and dipped it in. She licked the margarita from his erection, smacking her lips. She looked up and saw that his eyes were wide open. He lifted her up from her knees and drew her close to his warm, naked body, then reached down between her legs.

"Ooh, shit," he whispered. Her pussy was wet and with each stroke of his finger across her clit she became more excited. "Now it's your turn," he said. He led her through the darkened house to their bedroom and sat her on the edge of the bed. He laid her down on her back and spread her legs. Chills ran through her body when he buried his face in her pussy, his thick, full lips kissing her softly, gently, teasing her until she put her hands on the back of his head and pulled him closer. She moaned, her breath coming in quick, heavy gasps.

Then he introduced his tongue to the event. She came almost immediately, her legs trembling, and she involuntarily jerked away. He reached under and cupped her ass in his hands, pressing his tongue even deeper. Overwhelmed, she moved her pussy harder against his tongue. She loved the humming sound he made while he was between her legs. She closed her eyes to better feel his voice vibrating against the lips of her pussy.

She instinctively reached for his dick. He slid his muscular frame upward along her body until they were face to face. She held his penis in her hands and massaged it until a drop of cum ran from the tip. When she felt the moisture, she looked down at what they'd both agreed was the most beautiful dick she'd ever seen. It was the same delicious reddish brown as the rest of his body. She ran her fingers along the large vein that ran the length of his shaft, teasing him to near orgasm. He pushed his dick against her pelvic bone and she flinched at the pressure. She adjusted her body to redirect the head of his penis to the opening of her wet, pulsating pussy. He thanked her in kind by pushing himself into her hot moist center in one gliding motion. She moaned softly at first, then realized they were alone and shouted out his name. He stroked her pussy with an arrogance to which he had every right. He knew that he pleased her. She responded with a confidence of her own, rolling her hips up and around to greet every inch of him. He moaned her name over and over again, low, close to her ear.

"I wanna cum," she breathed out between his powerful thrusts.

"Then cum for me, Baby," he said, stroking faster. His voice reached out and sucked her nipples. She wished he'd say it again.

"Cum for me, Baby," he whispered into her ear. "Please, Baby," he whispered into her other ear. Had she wished out loud?

"I'm cumming," she said, her words coming in short, staccato bursts. "Here I cum."

"Can I cum with you?" he asked as if he needed her permission. She ground her hips harder and faster into his, hoping to cum again. And if he just kept licking the curve of her ear, whispering his sweet love, she knew that she would.

She slowed her pace, then pushed him onto his back. She straddled him, slowly lowering herself down onto his hard dick, pushing him deep inside her, swallowing more and more of him with every stroke. He began to push up into her as she pushed down into him.

"Are you ready, Baby?" he asked.

"Ready for what?" she asked, just to keep him talking.

"Are you ready for me to cum inside this fine, hot pussy," he panted.

"Oh, yes," she said.

"I'm cumming, Baby," his voice now louder, more intense. "Cum with me, Baby. Cum with me, now. Gimme all you got, Baby. Take all this dick. This is your dick, Baby, all yours." She felt his dick expand and jerk inside her and her pussy contracted tightly around it. "Oh, shit!" he yelled.

They came together, spasm after spasm, after spasm, after spasm, until she collapsed, trembling and out of breath, onto his chest. They lay quietly for a moment, relishing the silence until their heartbeats gradually returned to a normal pace.

"Do you think we can sell the kids?"

"We love the kids, remember?"

"Oh, right. I guess I'll just have to come home early more often," he said, smacking her on the ass. They laughed, then fell silent, locked in a warm embrace.

He thought about the time he'd come across her in the laundry room, bent over the hamper, sorting their dirty laundry. Her round firm ass seemed to beckon him. "Come on over here and feel this," it seemed to say. "Fuck me now. Here." But she had just gone off on him and the kids for taking their clothes off inside out, making more work for her. He didn't know how she'd react to his fantasy of lifting her onto the vibrating dryer or the washing machine during the spin cycle and fucking her brains out. But this weekend... the vibes were right, the kids were gone. He'd offer to help with the laundry.

She had stood on the back porch some weeks back and watched him mow the backyard. He'd stripped to the waist, sweat dripping from his forehead, his shoulders, down his back and hairless chest. When the sun had suddenly peeked from behind the expansive shade of the broad lemon tree that stood on the edge of their yard, the light glistened off his sweaty brow, his muscular back and strong arms. He glowed. She swooned. Didn't know whether to run to him and pull him down into the freshly mown grass or fetch him a glass of her world-famous homemade lemonade. But the kids and their friends were skirting the edges of the yard, playing tag. A roll in the grass seemed out of the question. But this weekend...

This weekend the kids were gone and after the recent rains, the grass was even taller then before he'd mowed it several weeks ago. She'd pick twenty or twenty-five lemons in the morning while the grits cooked and have a pitcher of fresh cold lemonade ready when she told him he needed to cut the grass. Once he'd stripped down to the waist, she'd strip down to the waist—and let him do the rest.

"Good night, Baby," he said, thinking back to the time when they made love against the cool tiles of the shower almost every morning—before the kids came.

"Good night," she murmured, remembering a long-ago night in the front seat of the car, the backseat of the car, just inside the front door, on the kitchen counter, in the dining room, up against the refrigerator, clothes littering the hallway all the way to the bed.

"See you in the morning," he whispered.

sex hall

MR Daniel

The hallway is narrow. I had expected it to be less bare—there are no pictures on the walls, which have all been painted dark reds, slick mahoganies, and purples. I laugh to myself. The colored girls must have had fun checking out swollen pussies when they were painting this. The lights are sunk deep into the ceiling and turned down low so it's lit like a club. A house diva is wailing through the PA system, backed up by an insistent fuck-me-baby, fuck-me-baby tempo. I feel as though I'm in a peepshow.

Brown, bronze, and various sun-kissed women move past me, some with their eyes straight forward, nervous, others whose eyes seem to burn a path before them. I can feel their heat as they pass. There is a steady pulsing below my skin as I move forward, the current stopping and starting and me feeling the blood push-flow push-flow through my neck and fingers, my heart growing, forcing blood into my breasts. I pass the first doorway and hesitate. The door is open but I am suddenly afraid to be caught looking.

Someone behind me stops to look over my shoulder, and her fingers inquire at my leg. I can feel her questions all the way up my thigh into my stomach. I almost jump into the room, and there is laughter behind me. I catch my breath, surprised at my confusion. This morning I was so sure of what I wanted, what I felt, but now... Excitement? Pleasure? Fear?

Didn't I want to be fucked from behind, anonymous?

A voice in my ear is saying, "Look forward, baby, or I'll leave."

And, "I know you're wet."

And, "When I remember how you look I'm going to think about parting your bush, how you *almost* reached behind to guide my hands. But I told you not to move. *Don't move.*"

Hiking up skirt, pulling down panties, the snap of a glove, and a hand between my legs. Fucked in a doorway. Fingers up my cunt, feeling the space in my flesh, pushing deeper and rubbing 'til there's this cross between a sharpness and pleasure, my muscles filled with blood, taut, filling and pressing until I think I'm going to pee on the floor.

My mouth is filled with stars and they're burning their way through my vagina. They hurl through my chest and I can't breathe; sweat collects in the band of my skirt. They light up nerves, sending shocks to my clit and behind my eyelids. I hear myself salivate as she works her hand in further, I pant, my cunt pants for her and the feeling of stars.

I am high, nipples sharp from the sound of her inside me. I am straining against damp fabric, pores fucked alert, open, wanting to feel air on sweat-and-oil-steeped skin, as I brace myself in the doorway.

Bodies passing by us go quiet as another finger goes in my puckering ass, tilted to receive, and lips circle my neck, her tongue leaving a trail that ends with a mouth clamped on the back of my throat, kissing, sucking hard, until a half-moon appears. I wanna come bad, but I could stay here forever.

Can you fuck too much? Can you feel too good? Can you be so ripe that you keep bursting and swelling, bursting and swelling until a mouth bites you open again? Her teeth burn into my ass, she whips the hand out of my cunt and I feel the air leave my chest, my breasts suddenly get heavy and full. Her hand spanks my ass, my skin wet and hot, and enters me again like horses. I swear I'm gonna drop to my knees as the finger in my ass moves back and forth, teasing the rim of my anus. I feel myself coming, raging against the horses, grasping them, expelling-thrusting them out as they lunge, push further inside. She holds onto me. "That hand isn't going anywhere," she says.

I feel come like hushed spurts, warm like blood, flowing out of me. I'm on my knees, my unconscious fingers take her horse hand, arching as I pull her out of me and rub her against my lips and clit. I feel like a dog, mouth open and bent over, writhing against her hand, I'm not thinking anymore, just doing what feels good. She doesn't pull away. I come again, air passes through my throat and I hear a sound like the last breath as you break the surface of water. Doubled over, breathing hard, I pull away from the finger in my ass and push her other hand from between my legs. I lick my juice from her glove, and pull the latex off. My tongue dives for the skin in between her fingers. This is how I will remember her, by her hands. She helps me up from behind, pulling up my panties stretched and tangled in my boots, her fingers spread wide feeling me up as she pulls my skirt down.

She bites my neck and says, "It's too bad you came so soon," and rubs her pelvis against the crack of my behind. I can feel her packing. Well, I'm sorry, too.

"Next time," she says, her hands firm on my hips, teasing, pressing into, circling against me, slowly. "It's underneath my black vinyl shorts, it peeks through a little cause they're short-shorts like the ones the reggae dancehall queens wear. Zippers up the sides. I only wear them here."

"How do you know you're the only one?" I ask. She can't see me smile.

"Well, if I'm not, we'll find out soon enough," she laughs, and bites the half-moon she left before. I listen to her walking away.

Boots, I guess, with heavy soles.

Five Hundred Dollars
Renée Swindle

I woke up having one of those mornings. The kind where instead of pressing the snooze button and praying for another five minutes of sleep, you simply turn the whole damn alarm off. Don't misunderstand, I wasn't in the habit of missing work. I showed up to both my jobs on time and ready to hustle. But on that particular morning, as I hugged my pillow to my chest and stared up into my bedroom ceiling, I knew there was just no way I could play receptionist all day, only to turn around and play waitress all night. So I called in sick. In my own gentle way, I told Boss Man Number One that he would have to make his own damn coffee for a change and answer his own damn phone calls. I told Boss Man Number Two that I had the flu. Did he really want to risk me passing out in the restaurant? Throwing up on somebody's food?

I didn't feel I was lying to either of them. I was sick. Sick of working so hard for so little. Sick of watching my days roll into each other without a single surprise, sick of feeling like my life had turned into nothing more than two simple phrases: How can I direct your call and May I take your order.

I didn't do much on my day off. Slept in past noon. Watched a few talk shows. I drove out to La Jolla for the hell of it and walked along the beach. You would've thought I had all the time in the world if you saw me. Just a woman staring out at the ocean. Just a woman taking a leisurely midday stroll. After my walk, I decided to browse through a few of the upscale boutiques that line the main boulevard, the kind where saleswomen with frozen blonde hair and ridged blue eyes follow your every move like you can't help but steal something. You are black, after all. But they were right to watch me, actually. I'm certainly no shoplifter, but I was tempted to take something. A silk bra. A gold bracelet. Some sort of souvenir from the world I'd always dreamed of living in.

Instead of shoplifting, I chose to use up a saleswoman's time by trying on expensive outfits I could never afford. One after another. A blouse made of silk organza. A pale blue satin skirt. A black cocktail dress with pearl inlays. Everything I put on made me feel like I was more than a waitress-slash-receptionist. More than a college dropout with a hundred and forty dollars in her checking account. More than a woman who hadn't had a single date in the past seven months. I didn't want to leave. I wanted to pretend that I lived in La Jolla and could afford something nice.

After the shops closed, I drove back to San Diego and caught a movie. After the movie I decided to treat myself to a drink. I figured why not celebrate my last few hours of illness? The closest bar was next to an out-of-business Laundromat and a ninety-nine-cent-Chinese-food restaurant. The neon sign over the bar flashed ANCERS. The *L* flicking on and off as though it were trying to stay alive.

The inside of the place was pretty much like you'd expect. Old barstools lined the bar. Cracked red vinyl booths sat along the opposite wall. There was a pool table and a dance floor big enough for two couples with a small disco ball overhead. A jukebox sat in one corner and next to the jukebox, an old white man with stringy gray hair wobbled from foot to foot. You couldn't tell if he was dancing or about to pass out. The few other people in the place didn't look much better. Ten or so old people staring into their glasses and nodding their heads to the country musiccoming from the jukebox. If I'd had any sense I would've kept walking, but I told myself that if I was tired of doing the same thing day-in and day-out, I needed to try new things. Why not hang out with a bunch of broken-down white folks and listen to country music? Yee ha!

I was taking a sip from my Long Island iced tea when a woman who looked to be in her sixties came over.

"Hey, are you a Sagittarius?"

"No."

"A Virgo?"

"No."

The woman took a sip of her drink, thinking for a moment. She had long lavender nails and matching lavender eye shadow that reached from the inside of her nose to the far end of her eyebrows. She wore a gold leotard that dipped in the front so that it showed off two heaping mounds of wrinkled cleavage. Her big Texas-style hair climbed into the air like a small mountain made from hair spray and bobby pins.

"I read fortunes. Your name start with a C?"

"No, an L. It's Leah."

"What, honey? I can't hear you with this country shit they're playing."

"Leee-ah."

"My name is Doris Ann. I'm a Capricorn and I'm fifty-four years old." She wiggled her shoulders so that her breasts shook. "I look pretty good, huh?" She pointed at the jukebox with one of her long nails. "I'm gonna play something just for you. Gotta quarter?"

I gave her a quarter and watched her saunter over to the jukebox. The Ojays came on a few seconds later and she shot her fist in the air. "That's better, huh?" She lifted her glass and I clinked mine to hers. "Hey, are you a teacher? I'm picking up on you being a teacher."

I had to laugh. She was a lousy fortune-teller. "No, I'm a waitress. A waitress and a receptionist."

"Get outta here. I'm a waitress too. A waitress and a fortune-teller. I've been waitin' tables since I was sixteen! Ain't that somethin'? Forty years of bustin' my ass and askin' people what they want to eat. I make good money telling fortunes. I can't ever tell what's going to happen to me, though. Ain't that somethin'?"

I looked her over then. Saw myself forty years later. A black version of Doris Ann. Old. Lonely. Still waiting tables and trying to tell my own fortune.

I downed my drink and asked for another.

Doris Ann and I were swapping waitressing stories, trying to outdo each other with our all-time-worst experiences when she tapped my arm. "Look what we got here," she said, nodding her head toward the entrance.

A man stood in the doorway. While I couldn't tell if he was Puerto Rican or what, his dark brown skin definitely gave off the fact that he had some African blood running through his veins. He was much older than me, not my taste at all, but I liked how his chest muscles stretched against his leather jacket. I liked the way he looked over his cigarette at everyone in the bar like they were beneath him. And I was all too happy to see some color in the place.

Doris Ann started her fortune-telling routine as soon as he found a seat at the bar. "Hey, buddy, your name start with a M?"

"Excuse me?"

Doris Ann turned to me, her eyes big. "Hear that, Leah? Our new friend here has an accent. Where you from, huh?"

"I'm from America."

"How can you be from America if you have an accent? You from Mexico or somethin'?"

The man and I rolled our eyes at the same time and I smiled. He was good-looking for an older man. Nice lips, even caramel-brown skin, and although his hair was buried under a layer of gel, it was thick and jet black. He had wrinkles around his eyes and forehead, but he had a build like a boxer's and gave off the impression that he could kick some serious ass if he wanted to.

After ordering his drink and lighting a cigarette, he asked if he could buy Doris Ann and me another round.

"Ooh, we've finally got us a gentleman in this dump," Doris Ann said. "I always say foreigners are nicer."

After the bartender served our drinks, the man moved over two seats and introduced himself. "I'm George."

I shook his hand. "Nice to meet you. I'm Leah."

Doris Ann lifted her shot of tequila. "I'm Doris Ann! Cheers, everybody!"

I rested my elbow on the bar. I could feel a nice buzz coming on and didn't really care if I was leaning in too close. "You don't look like a George at all."

"That's because his name starts with an M," Doris Ann said with a belch. "I can feel it."

"I'll prove I'm telling the truth." He was about to open his wallet when I playfully snatched it away. I paused when I realized how heavy it felt. Before he could stop me, I opened the side of the wallet and took a peek at the bills. There were a few fifties but the rest of the bills were hundreds. One after the other after the other.

I leaned in closer and folded my hands next to my cheek. "What the hell did you do, rob a bank?"

"I thought you were interested in my name."

I opened the wallet again and looked at the driver's license. Jorge Morales. I smiled over at Doris Ann. "He's telling the truth. Sort of."

I handed over his wallet with a smirk. "What did you do to make all that money, George?"

"That's a secret."

"Come on, you can tell me."

Doris Ann took a step toward us, her head wobbling a bit. "I have a feeling that money is dirty. I can feel it."

I raised my eyebrows at George. "Is she right?"

He shrugged slightly, lifting his shoulder as if to dismiss the subject.

A man dressed in brown corduroy pants and a beige corduroy jacket came over and asked Doris Ann if she wanted to dance.

"Hot damn! 'Bout time somebody noticed me around here." She took the man's hand and they headed off to the tiny dance floor.

I turned to George. "So where'd you get all the money? You don't have to be so secretive. I won't tell."

George studied me carefully, gazing at my hair and face. "How old are you, Leah?"

"Twenty-six."

"Twenty-six." He shook his head as though my age was bad news. "You are lovely, Miss Leah. But you probably have men telling you that all the time."

Actually I couldn't remember the last time a man gave me a nice compliment. Usually some ass would leave his telephone number at my table along with a so-so tip. Or I'd be filing something at the real estate office, turn around, and see some old bastard checking me out.

George stared at the bottles behind the bar. As he took a last hit from his cigarette, I noticed a small mole high up near his cheekbone. "I would love to cook dinner for you. Why don't you come to my place and I'll make a nice dish from the Dominican. *Arroz con habichuelas. Pollo guisado.* All delicious."

"Nuh-uh. No way. You could take me home and make me for dinner."

"I don't want to hurt you. I want to cook for you."

"I don't think so."

We were quiet again before he asked if he could buy me another drink. When he took out his wallet I eyed all those bills. What must it be like to have your wallet full of money like that? I wondered. What must it feel like not to have to count every fucking penny? He tapped his glass to mine when the drinks arrived then rested his hand on his hip and watched me take a sip of my drink. "I really think you are beautiful. No bullshit. I understand that you don't want to come to my place. Why don't you allow me to take you out? I'll take you someplace nice."

I took another sip and looked around the bar. A few more people had trickled in, but the place was far from full. I glanced over at Doris Ann. She had her arm hanging over Corduroy's shoulder and the two dipped and swayed to an '80s pop song. I pictured her at the restaurant where she worked, dressed in a pink apron, carrying a pad and pencil. *I've been waitin' tables since I was sixteen!* Tomorrow, I knew, I'd be doing the same thing. Come six o'clock after the four hours I put in at the real estate office, I'd be hustling for tips. I turned to George and glanced down at his wallet, which he'd sat next to his drink. The offer for dinner was nice and all, but I was more interested in money—his money. What was the difference, really, between hustling for a tip and maybe trying to get George to share a little bit of his wealth? What was wrong with seeing how much I could get?

And so I put my hand on his thigh, leaned in so that our lips almost touched. "I have an idea."

"What's that?"

"I'll give you a kiss if you give me one of those bills in your wallet."

I figured all he had to do was say no. And to be honest, a large part of me expected him to say no.

But he didn't. He kept his face close to mine as he slowly reached for his wallet and pulled out a fifty-dollar bill. Just like that. Fifty dollars for a kiss.

I smiled as I took the bill, waved it in the air. "Really?" He nodded yes.

So I moved in and pressed my lips against his and then because, hell, he'd given me fifty dollars, I parted his lips with my tongue, sliding it into his mouth and wrapping it around his, letting it feel the tip then pressing it deep inside his mouth.

We pulled apart after Doris Ann yelled out from the dance floor. The Ojays were playing again and she was sticking her finger in the air like John Travolta in *Saturday Night Fever.*

I was staring down at the fifty when George touched the side of my bare arm with the tip of his fingers and brushed lightly back and forth. "Come home with me." Now that we had kissed I noticed his lips were better than nice. They were beautiful, really. Full, almost pouty.

I kissed the mole on his cheek. "You're too old for me," I teased.

He leaned back and grinned. "What does age have to do with sharing a bottle of good wine and food?"

But I wanted to keep playing kissing for dollars. The combination of easy money, alcohol, and a man who knew how to kiss was more of a thrill than I thought it would be. Something about getting that fifty made me feel better than I had in a while. Confident. Sexy. Besides, the first fifty was so easy, why stop now?

I crossed my legs so that my skirt rose up across my brown thighs, then leaned over and traced his ear with my tongue, slowly following along the edge, letting it leave a wet trail. "Instead of dinner, how about another kiss?"

George held my face between his hands and began covering me with soft, light kisses. When he moved toward my lips I pushed him away. "No, no. That's not what I meant." I rubbed my fingers in the air as a hint. "Like last time," I said.

His small brown eyes studied mine. When he saw that I was serious he went for his wallet and took out another fifty. He put it in my hand and held it there before bringing my hand to his lips and kissing it softly.

"Thank you."

"Yes, but what about my kiss?"

I smiled and put my arms around him. We kissed harder this time. Our tongues searching each other's mouths. When I could feel his hands on my waist, gripping me as though, if he could, he'd pick me up and sit me on his lap, I pulled back and whispered against his ear. "I'll tell you what. Give me a hundred and I'll let you put your finger inside me."

He kept his hands on my waist and touched his forehead to mine. "I really want to have dinner with you. We don't have to play these games."

"I know you want to."

He shook his head slightly.

But the alcohol was helping me feel bold and brave. I took his hand and led him to the booth furthest away from the door. After we sat down, I looked around the bar to make sure no one was watching and then hiked my skirt up so he could see my black panties, so he could see me move my panties over and glide my finger deep inside my vagina. My finger glistened after I pulled it out. I gave it a wiggle then ran it from the top of his forehead to just under his nose until he closed his eyes and inhaled.

He took out a bill and handed it to me before taking my finger and putting it in his mouth, sucking on it with closed eyes.

I looked around the bar again. Heads stared down into drinks. A couple moved together on the dance floor. Doris Ann was playing pool with Corduroy as another man watched. I took George's hand and moved it toward my waist. He kissed the side of my face as he pulled my panties aside with the hook of his finger then slowly slid his finger inside me. I tried my best to keep my eyes open, to watch him watching me, but once I felt his finger I let my head fall back. I was almost embarrassed at how wet I was. It had been so long, my body felt like it was made of nothing more than a single aching need.

"Do you like that?" he said, pushing his thick finger in deeper. He slipped another finger in and glided them both in and out with a steady pressure. He kissed my neck as I tried my best to rock my hips against the rhythm of his fingers. I was surprised by how much I wanted him.

"I want to taste your pussy," he whispered. "I want to taste you in my mouth."

I opened my eyes and held his chin in my hand. "Two hundred."

He took out two bills and held them up in the air. "Fine."

I snatched the money before he could change his mind then stood and motioned toward the door.

Doris Ann was still playing pool as we made our way out. "You leavin' already?"

"No," I said over the awful music. "Just getting some fresh air."

I led George out to the parking lot. The cold air helped me come off my buzz some, but I was definitely drunk. There was a single light over the back door of the Chinese restaurant, but it wasn't bright enough to light the entire parking lot. Five or six cars were parked here and there. George and I hid in the back between a brick wall and a delivery truck with Chinese lettering. The only way we could be seen was if someone stood directly in front of us.

George kept his face directly in front of mine as he drove his hands under my blouse, lifting my bra so that he could run his cool fingertips over my breasts. When he felt my nipples harden, he unlatched my bra and took both my breasts in his hands, squeezing and caressing them. When he felt my body begin to sway, he got on his knees and lifted my skirt. He rubbed my thighs and ass while staring up into my face and then finally began to roll my panties down my legs, slowly, carefully, as if I were a delicacy he wanted to savor.

He paused when he saw me naked like that. "My God," he said. "My God." And then he buried his face in my pubic hair, taking a long deep breath before finally pressing his tongue against my clitoris. I clutched the bills he'd given me in one hand and with the other held the back of his head, running my fingers through his thick hair. He moved his tongue inside me, pushing in deeper and deeper while using a finger to play with my clit. He used his finger and tongue until I could feel myself on the verge of coming. "Jorge," I said, my voice sounding far, far away. "Jorge…I…"

He stood up and pressed his body into mine. His breath was hot against my face and smelled of gin. "What?" he asked, kissing my neck. "What, Leah? Tell me." I could feel his cold belt buckle against my bare stomach, his erection pushing itself against my naked pelvis. I wanted to say that I wanted more. I wanted to say that I wanted to feel him inside of me. I wanted to say I'd never had it so good. But instead I tried my best to catch my breath, to gather my thoughts. He put both hands up against the wall as though he were trapping me. "What were you going to say, Miss Leah?"

I unzipped his pants, pressed my hand against his stomach and carefully slid it down the inside of his underwear so I could wrap it around his penis. I started kissing his neck, inhaling his musk cologne. "I was going to ask if you want more."

I could feel his penis throbbing inside my hand, thick, warm, and then he let his body move forward, his mouth ready to kiss me. "Yeah, I want more. How much, huh? How much does it cost to fuck you?"

I ran my thumb over the tip of his penis and kissed him lightly on the lips. "Another two."

He took a step back then. His shirt was coming out of his pants, his hair disheveled, but he looked handsome in that parking lot. The night shadows cutting across his face. "Okay," he whispered. He moved forward again and this time took my breasts in his hands with more force, reaching down and kissing them, sucking hard on one nipple and then the other. I let my head fall back so that I was staring straight up into the dark sky. My mouth fell open, my hands scraped against the brick wall searching for something to grasp. I let out a moan and then pulled his underwear down and stroked his penis faster and then faster still. He slid a finger inside me, then another. His breath was measured and quiet, but then he said something in Spanish and turned me around so that my back was to him. He licked my ear before bending me over, before running his soft nails down my back. He cupped my breasts and pressed his pelvis against my ass. I reached back and pulled at his thighs, then spread my legs apart to urge him inside. I heard him fumbling with something and realized he was putting on a condom. When it was on, he knelt down and spread my legs even further. He stared at my wet sex before licking it, kissing it, before pulling my butt cheeks apart and licking harder.

"Do you want me inside of you?"

I wiggled my ass in his face. "Yeah, Jorge. Yeah."

He stood and cupped my breasts, ran his tongue up my back and then placed his hands at my hips. He pushed his entire penis inside of me with one hard thrust. He gripped me tighter at the waist so he could pull my body into his, pushing his penis in and out with full force. My entire body was upside down, my hair falling over, my fingertips brushing against the asphalt. All I could feel was his cock pushing deeper, faster, harder. And that was all I wanted to feel. I was moaning, in fact, moaning so loud he had to cover my mouth.

He turned me around suddenly and in one motion picked me up high in the air, nudging my legs so that I knew to wrap them around his waist. When I did, he lifted me up onto his penis then pulled me down. I buried my face in his neck and let out a whimper as I felt him inside me again. The new position made his penis feel longer, thicker. I wrapped my arms tightly around his neck and shoulders as he lifted me up and brought me down, bringing my body again and again against his penis. I put my hand over my mouth when I felt myself coming and let out a muffled moan. But George didn't stop. He kept going, lifting me up and down until he took my breasts in his mouth and sucked hard on my nipple. He swung me up again and our heads fell back at the same time. I felt his penis quiver inside me as he let my body fall against his one last time.

We stood like that, me up in his arms, my head buried in his neck, breathing in unison like worn-out dancers afraid to pull apart. But then we heard Doris Ann's voice coming from the edge of the parking lot. "Hey, Leah, are you back there? Something was telling me you might need my help."

Our bodies began to untwine, moving slowly as though we were finally remembering where we were, remembering that we were in a parking lot behind a bar, two people who hardly knew each other. George let me go and we both started straightening our clothes.

Doris Ann spoke loudly this time. "Is that you back there? You okay?"

"Yeah, Doris Ann, I'm fine. I had to get some air."

George was shaking his head as he tucked in his shirt. "I wanted dinner, you know?" he said, half chuckling. "I thought you were beautiful and wanted to do something nice." A part of me wanted to suggest that we still could have dinner together, but he went for his wallet and took out two bills. He shoved the bills into my hands and then held my arm so that I would look at him. "I would've paid you more," he said. "Much more." And then he walked away.

Doris Ann was still there when I walked out. Her eye shadow had faded and her eyeliner formed black bags under her eyes. "Are you okay?"

I laughed a little. "Yeah, I'm fine."

"You shouldn't just wander off with strangers, you know. You get in trouble like that." She stared down at my blouse, which hung loosely around my body, and then looked out toward the street. "It's dangerous. You could get hurt or something."

"I'm fine," I said, trying to smile.

"Well, I'm going to get going. Long day tomorrow. I've got the morning shift. I shouldn't be here at all if I had any sense." She turned to leave. "Good night, Leah."

I watched her walk out of the parking lot. Then I remembered the money. I took out all the bills George had given me, straightened them out nice and neat.

Five hundred dollars.

I already knew how I was going to spend it, too. I was going to call in sick again, drive out to La Jolla. But this time I was going to be one of the lucky ones.

Two Heads Are Better Than One
Karen Johnson

"Put down the dick and back away from the pussy," Mona said to Veronica, her new neighbor and colleague.

Veronica had picked up the large wooden penis from Mona's desk and was stroking the stuffed black cat with the other hand.

That morning when they'd entered the same elevator at the Glass and Gleam Towers, Veronica had pushed the button for the thirty-third floor. Mona knew then that Veronica must be the new sex therapist with whom she'd be sharing a receptionist and an adjoining office. She introduced herself and invited Veronica to stop by her office before settling in. When they got off the elevator, the women stopped at the reception desk so that Mona could introduce Veronica to Marie, the receptionist, and check her messages. Then they walked down the carpeted hallway to Mona's spacious office.

Veronica admired Mona's fuchsia walls, her file-laden mahogany desk, the sumptuous leather furniture, and the bookcase-lined walls. She walked across the deep red-brown carpet to the large palm tree that stood at the window. "Nice view," she said, then noticed the "toys" on Mona's desk.

She fondled the wooden penis, sculpted to favor a huge mushroom with a fat stem. "This is nice. Who's the artist?" Veronica asked.

"I forget her name," Mona said. "But I do remember that she carved it with her buck teeth!"

"More importantly," Veronica asked, "who's the model?"

"If I knew who he was I wouldn't be working here. I'd be working on that—and vice versa."

"I think I'd call this piece—and the model—'Night and Day,' and I think I'd call often," Veronica said. They shared a laugh, and Veronica looked contemplatively at the oversized dick. "Each one has two heads. All thought begins at the high one and ends at the low one. That triggers the renewal of the brain cells."

"Damn," Mona said. "You're deep for a sex therapist. Been thinking about it for a while, eh?"

"Well, I don't want to wear it out," Veronica said, returning the sculpture to its upright position on the desk.

"It's oak," Mona told her. "You can't wear it out."

Veronica picked up the smiling, life-sized, nylon-furred, stuffed black cat from its post next to the dick. "Subtle," she said. "Don't these props scare off your clients?"

"Just the half that doesn't like sex," Mona replied. "I used to have nightmares of being drowned by the rape victims." The split-second image of a girl being thrown onto the ground passed silently between the women.

"If you ever want to talk about it, I know a good therapist," Veronica offered. She replaced the pussy and picked up a large fan-shaped seashell. "Explain this."

"Tits," Mona said. "And if you ever need help getting out of the deep and onto the shore, I'll throw *you* a line."

Veronica lifted the shell to her left ear and grabbed the wooden penis with her right hand, holding it to her mouth as though the dick-and-shell set were an old-time telephone. "You gotta help me, Doc! I can't get through to my clit!"

Mona laughed and shook her head from side to side. "You're a mess! I can't wait to see how *your* office is decorated."

The two building-maintenance men who were sitting on Veronica's deep brown leather sofa quickly jumped to attention when the women entered the office. "Damn! It looks like a forest in here." Mona exclaimed.

"We took the liberty of painting the 'fade' into the ceiling," the taller man said. "When we looked at your instructions, we figured, with the trees and everything, you were trying to make it natural. So we faded the blues." The ceiling had been painted night-blue and faded to a day-blue on the walls.

Veronica's jaw dropped in awe as her eyes scanned the walls from top to bottom.

"But," the shorter man assured, "if you don't like it, we'll paint it whatever way you say. We were just waiting for you and they said you were on your way so…we just waited to see what you thought."

"It's better than I'd hoped," Veronica said. "I love it! Thank you." She instructed the men on where to place her trees: one behind the couch, another by her desk at the window. The final two trees were placed on either side of a large painting that faced the sofa. The two men, elated that she had complimented their initiative and creativity in painting her office, moved swiftly, eager to please once more.

"Oh," Veronica said, "you put my books up on the shelves. I had a very specific order in mind." Disappointment slowed the work of the men and dulled the light in their eyes.

Mona nudged Veronica. "Hey, control freak," Mona whispered, "that's a whole lot of books they put up for you. Why don't you let them keep their joy?"

"But they're not in order," Veronica whined. She sighed with exasperation at the thought of how long it was going to take to redo the bookshelves.

"In what order do you put the feelings of others?" Mona asked. "What are all these books worth if you don't know that?"

"Of course you're right," Veronica said. She surveyed her beloved library, running her fingers over the spines of the books as she approached the maintenance men. "Actually," she said, "the order is very natural. I'm so grateful to you."

The men finished their work and left beaming with pride. Mona fetched champagne and two flutes from her office and the women celebrated their newfound friendship. Mona raised her glass to the six-by-five-foot painting of large red beach balls framed by the two trees. "Hope you get your wish," Mona toasted.

"And to all a good night," Veronica added as she tinked Mona's glass.

And so their friendship began. The women shared the light for two more years. Veronica considered installing a window between their offices, but realized they only needed a mirror. They had each developed the other's voice inside. Mona had so many "This is it. I know it in my heart!" romances that Veronica started calling her "Whore-Moan-a." And Veronica found so many "disorders" in the men she dated that Mona called her "Veronica-Never-Knew."

One morning Mona walked dazed into Veronica's office and, sighing deeply, told her about her three-hour-old romance with the fine, fine, superfine LaShawn Monroe. Mr. Fine, the producer of the hit TV series *The Couch,* employed Mona as a consultant. Mona had always found him to be distracted, fretting about this or that, and unapproachable. A high-strung stiff-ass—though a fine ass it was, she'd told Veronica. Everyone knew he was a fool for Deborah Dawson, the star of the series, who dangled LaShawn from a chain like a charm on a bracelet.

"I can't believe it," Mona said. "Just this morning I was fantasizing about me and Mr. Monroe making love in his studio office when Marie buzzed me to say he was at her desk asking to see me immediately. I thought I was in trouble or something. So I buzz him in and he strides in babbling something about 'Sorry to barge into your day like this, Mona.' Then he tells me how he's admired my expertise as a therapist and was hoping that I could help him with something that's been troubling him for a while.

"He didn't stop talking long enough for me to say yea or nay. He swooped by my desk and picked up the kitty on his way to the couch. He sits down and starts spilling his soul about how he's afraid that he's oversexed! Girl, I shot up a silent prayer like a rocket on a mission! He says he wants to fuck three times a day—at least—but Deborah gets tired seven days a week." Mona paused to catch her breath.

"I don't know what else he said, because he was absent-mindedly stroking the cat, and I couldn't concentrate. I'm seeing us fuck in his office. I'm seeing us fucking in his car all the way to his house, then all up in the house, then fucking on the way out of the house. I'm picturing us rolling around outside in a forest. Well, all of a sudden, he stopped talking like he was wondering if he left something cooking on the stove. Then he turns the cat upside down like he's checking to see if it's male or female, and sniffs the kitty's pussy!"

"Tell me this is not going where I think it's going," Veronica said.

"Then he says something about how not making love is like letting the sun go down without holding on to a *piece* of it. I'm thinking, 'Damn! He's a poet and I wish he'd hold on to a piece of my ass!' " Mona took a deep breath. "So I locked the door with the remote."

"No, you didn't! You fucked him? He's your employer!" Veronica's eyebrows didn't rise as far as her curiosity, though. "So then what happened?"

"Employer, schmoyer. I've wanted to bite him for two years. I couldn't take it anymore. I walked over to the couch, sat next to him, took the cat, and tossed it across the room. I lifted my skirt and lap-danced him. Oh, God, Veronica. This is it!"

"Again," Veronica warned. "Just how long do you think it's gonna last?"

A month later, Mona announced that she and LaShawn would be moving to New York in two weeks. "Hope I'm too busy fucking to miss you," Mona said, "but you know I will." The women hugged, then cried, then smiled at each other and hugged some more.

"You'll be too busy fucking to remember anything. Good for you!" Veronica said.

A year later, Mona called Veronica to tell her that she and LaShawn would be on the West Coast in a few days and that she had a big surprise.

"Hi, Ho!" someone shouted at Veronica's back at the airport. Veronica turned to face her old friend, the now-pregnant Mrs. Fine.

"Why, thank you!" Veronica said. They hugged and kissed and looked one another over, up and down, back and front. "You are definitely pregnant," Veronica said, "and you're glowing! I'm so happy for you. Where's the baby daddy?"

"He's getting the luggage. And who's got you smiling like you finally got a clue?" Mona asked, noting a marked transformation in Veronica's attitude and appearance. "You look great. No. You look *satisfied*."

"Listen, I'll get you guys settled at the hotel, then tomorrow I want you both to come out to our place at the lake. I can't wait for you to meet Frederick."

"Frederick?" Mona asked, one eyebrow raised in mock suspicion.

Veronica leaned across Mona's burgeoning belly to whisper, "I call him 'Frederick, the Fantastic Dick!'"

LaShawn and Mona followed Veronica's directions to the picturesque road that wound around the lake and led them to the circular driveway in front of Veronica and Frederick's large rustic home.

Veronica and Fred greeted them and ushered them to the shaded back porch that overlooked the lake. Veronica retreated to the kitchen and brought out a pitcher of lemonade. Fred and LaShawn hit it off immediately and excused themselves to go inside and watch a football game on TV. The women watched the men disappear beyond the screen door and listened for the sound of the television.

"Damn!" Mona said in a low voice, "where'd you meet him? I'll bet you have a hard time walking in the morning. I see you like 'em fine *and* short!"

"Yeah, but he's got a long ladder!" The women laughed and shared a low five. "You remember Dr. Durant? Well, he introduced us at a party to celebrate the completion of his new house. Fred was the landscape architect. He does wonderful things with wood and flowers, and..."

"Damn it! Where's the remote?" Fred banged the screen door and barged onto the porch. Before Mona could give Veronica a "what's-a-good-ex-sex-therapist-like-you-doing-in-a-confrontational-relationship-like-this" look, Veronica had shot up and gone into the house to "fetch." Mona made a mental note to talk to her docile friend, then found herself slipping into the vast beauty of the scenery.

The porch faced a huge oak tree that triumphed over the view about fifty feet from the porch and about a quarter-mile from the crystal blue lake. The oak's trunk curved dramatically to the left like a question mark, and the branches continued the curve, almost touching the ground. Mona's view of the lake through the curve of the tree was dizzying. The birds that darted about, and the lake itself, were distorted by the ninety-degree heat that rose from the ground in sweltering waves. The fragrance of some sweet-smelling flora wafted around the porch.

Mona's peaceful drifting was interrupted when she heard a sportscaster announce the first-quarter score. "What was that all about? What's up with the temper tantrum shit?" Mona asked when Veronica returned. "What is he, an 'artiste' or something?"

"There's nothing really wrong," Veronica assured her. "He just needed some stroking." She fanned the skirt of her flowered cotton summer dress, bringing cool relief to her sweaty thighs. "So, we're at this party at Dr. Durant's and Fred has done all of this gorgeous landscaping. Did I tell you that he used to be an architect?"

"What does he do now?" Mona asked, a little annoyed at her friend's nonchalant response to Fred's behavior.

"He, ah...he sculpts!" Veronica told Mona told about first meeting Fred and how he gave her a body scan from across the room. Dr. Durant had picked up on the attraction, introduced them, and left them alone to engage in polite conversation.

"Well, I could see that Fred wasn't listening to me. He was just kinda looking through me. And then he says, 'Would you like to go out for breakfast with me?' I totally forgot what I was talking about and said 'yes.' Then he says, 'Saturday morning, seven o'clock. Dress for the outdoors. I'll pick you up.' He gives me an X-ray smile and leaves the party!

"I got pissed because he didn't even wait to hear my answer. How'd he know whether I was available, or wanted to get up that early on a Saturday morning, or dress for the outdoors for breakfast? Well, *he's* an arrogant bastard, I thought. But I left the party wondering what 'the outdoors' meant and what I'd wear. I went home and pulled out all my leather clothes.

"I didn't have to wake up early Saturday 'cause I couldn't sleep Friday night. The man mesmerized me! I was ready at five, he showed up at six, and we drove out here, into the woods, talking and laughing the whole way. When we get to this spot, he starts unloading all this shit from the trunk of his car: sleeping bags, fishing poles, a camp stove, even a fucking tent! There was enough gear to live in the woods for a week.

"Had I told him I would spend the night? No! So I give him a look and he says, 'Could you lift something, please?' Next thing I know, we're putting up the tent. I put one sleeping bag on one side of the tent and one on the other side. You should have seen the look on his face. 'Don't worry,' he tells me, 'I won't fuck you unless you beg me!'"

"No, he didn't?" Mona said.

"Yes, he did! I told him I didn't have to beg for any goddamn thing in this life or the next, and maybe he should consider sleeping outside since his head might be too swelled to get into the tent. The whole time he's smiling this Cheshire-cat smile and I'm wondering if he's a fucking psycho."

"You're wondering if *he's* psycho?" Mona said in amazement. "I'm wondering if *you'd* gone over the edge. A man you've known for less than twenty-four hours asks you out to breakfast and you wind up in the woods putting up a tent and sleeping bags!"

"Well then he takes my hand and walks me out of the tent. He starts talking about how the birds love this time of the day so much that they sing. I don't know how to explain it, Mona. But when he picked up the fishing poles and started toward the lake, I followed him like a hungry puppy." Veronica lowered her voice and glanced back at the screen door. "We get to the lake and Fred says, 'You'll have to take off your pants unless you plan to get that leather wet.' My panties were already so wet, I thought my period had started—after three years! 'How could I have planned anything when you failed to mention that we'd be *catching* breakfast?' I said. He just smiled and took off his pants. He was wearing swimming trunks. I was wearing a thong! I took off my pants and waded out into the lake with him, thinking that if he didn't get more considerate soon, this would be the first and last date.

"Okay, so now we're both in about three feet of water with our poles dangling in the lake. 'What exactly is it we're trying to catch?' I ask him. 'Catfish,' he says. 'Aren't catfish too slimy to be in clear water like this?' I ask. 'Let me show you how to do it,' he says. He comes up behind me and nozzles his mushroom up against my butt. Now this is more like it, I think. He drops his pole in the water and he's massaging my tits until I'm so dizzy, I drop my pole. When I reach down to pick it up, he grabs me around the waist and works his thing into my coochie 'til my knees buckle.

"Then—just like that—he drops me face down into the water!"

"No!" Mona said.

"Yes!" Veronica said. "Then he picks up his pole and walks back to the shore, and without even looking back at me, he says, 'I told you that you'd have to beg for it.' "

"Shit!" squealed Mona.

"No shit," said Veronica. "Now I'm coughing lake water, my suede top is ruined, my ego popped, and I'm steaming! I charged through the water after him and dove for his legs. I knocked him back on his ass and we both lay there brushing off dirt and leaves, glaring at each other. When he stood up over me, I thought, 'Shit! He *is* a psycho!' He lifted me two feet in the air and put me down in front of a tree. I guess he took my knocking him to the ground as begging, because he commenced to fuck me roy-al-ly.

"No!"

"Oh, yes! He grinded me slowly at first like he knew where the spark in my clit was going to hit and he was there to meet it! My ass became one with the tree. He licked my nipples until my head ding-donged, then went down on me, stopping along the way like he was wondering if he should go further. Girl, I merged with every ring in the tree all the way back to when it was a sapling! He caught all the small fires between my legs until they roared up in one big flame. I'm telling you, my brain was singing, 'Happy birthday to me. Happy birthday to me. Happy BIRTHDAY, dear Veronica. Happy birthday to me!' The tree was moaning and singing along with me."

Silence. Both women stared, not seeing, toward the warm oranges and reds of the setting sun on the lake's surface.

"And now?" Mona asked. "Did he keep it up after that first date?"

"See that tree?" Veronica nodded at the question-marked trunk of the big oak tree. "It used to be straight."

"Dang." Mona laughed. She raised her glass in a toast, as the laughter from the house announced that the men would soon return. "Here's to the curve."

"To the curve...," Veronica clinked her glass against Mona's, "...and to the big head and the little head."

The Teddy Boys

B. P. Jones

Sara stopped at her mailbox as she came in from tutoring her literacy student, Delilah. She and Delilah were the same age—fifty-one—and it amazed Sara that Delilah could've lived so long without really knowing how to read. Sara felt that she would not have the courage and stamina to take on such a task at their age. "You go, girl," she thought.

When Sara got inside her home, took off her coat, and put her feet up, she thumbed through the mail. A letter, post-marked Philadelphia, stood out from the gas bill and the standard junk mail. Who, she thought, do I know in Philly?

Hey, girl. It's been way too long. I hope this is still a good address for you. The opening didn't clue Sara in, so she looked at the signature at the bottom of the third page: Your partner in seduction, Carolyn. A smile of recognition and a little bit more spread across Sara's face. She went back to the top of the letter.

I'm here in the so-called City of Brotherly Love, although I can't find a brother to love for the life of me! I sure do miss Oakland. Girl, you don't know how I wish I'd never left.

I was going through some of my things on my birthday and I suddenly remembered that movie The Bridges of Madison County. *I didn't want my poor children to discover any shockers when it comes time for them to sort through the effects of their dear departed, saintly, and, I might add—except for them—virginal mother.*

Sara laughed out loud. It was Carolyn Green. Leave it to her to make a joke out of their mortality.

True enough, guess what I found in an old shoebox? An old journal with an entry about that night and—are you ready?—THE garter belt! I must have laughed for the rest of the day, then I discreetly removed them to a place where they would never be found, but I could still get to them when I needed a good laugh.

Girl, do you realize that was seventeen years ago? Seventeen years! I simply refuse to believe it. But I'd written the date right there at the top of the page—September 7, 1984, like I was trying to make sure I would incriminate myself. I just had to touch base and rekindle the old memory cells for you. I may eventually forget my phone number, my address, who knows, maybe even my name. But I will never forget that night. Your partner in seduction, Carolyn.

Carolyn. Sara was laughing by the time she got to the end of the letter. She'd forgotten how much she'd missed her friend when Carolyn moved back east. Was it really seventeen years ago? It didn't seem like more than ten.

It was a Friday night, Sara recalled. Carolyn had called her to meet at a local watering hole for an end-of-the-week, in Carolyn's words, "Thank God, Mary, Jesus, Joseph, and Mary Magdalene it's Friday" drink. They were in their thirties—fine, fit, single, and at that blissful stage in a woman's life when she knows she's got it together. Carolyn was the head-turner of the two—tall, slender, with a smooth copper brown complexion, high cheekbones, and exotic almond-shaped eyes. She was wearing braids then, cascading down her long neck to her shoulders. That night she had on a lavender pantsuit and high heels to show off her height.

When Sara walked into the bar, she spotted Carolyn in a seat at the outside corner. That was Carolyn's favorite perch, where she could see and be seen. Sara could tell Carolyn had just arrived; she could see and feel Carolyn's wake in the turned heads and agitated atmosphere that trails a stunning woman.

Sara didn't have that effect and she didn't want to. She enjoyed a more subtle attractiveness. She was medium height, medium light brown with dreamy dark brown eyes and an intriguing lopsided smile. Back then she was wearing her hair texturized-curly in one of those asymmetrical cuts that were all the rage in the mid-'80s. That night she still had on clothes from work, a charcoal brown suit with a skirt. She had a nice figure, but she dressed conservatively. It wasn't that she was a wallflower, not by a long shot. She just liked to be in control of who—make that whom—she attracted and when. Brothers often mistook her subdued appearance, thinking she was their long-lost virginal sweetheart. Boy did they get a rude awakening.

Carolyn moved her large leather purse from the stool next to her as Sara approached. They hugged and Sara sat down.

"Girl, I thought this week would never ever come to an end. The white people must have had a Klan convention last weekend because they were in high whiteness all week," Carolyn said. She was the only—the onliest, as she said—sister at an advertising firm in downtown San Francisco.

"I know just how you feel," Sara said. "But it was another sister I thought I was going to have to strangle this week. This lovely lady decided she was going to make some brownie points by trying to clown me." Sara was a systems analyst for Alameda County's health department.

"So what did you do?"

"I haven't done it yet. But if this oh-so-lovely lady continues to mess with me, there's a booby trap waiting to blow up in her fat, cross-eyed, look-like-the-cat-drug-it-in face."

"Whew, girl!" Carolyn gave her a high five and laughed. She got the bartender's attention and they ordered drinks. Carolyn was drinking Kir, as always. Sara ordered a margarita. The place was packed. They were lucky to have seats at the bar. They weren't the only ones celebrating the end of the week. And for this age group, every Friday was an excuse to go out on the prowl.

People were crammed everywhere—chairs crowded around small tables, bodies squeezed in around bar stools. The sound of dozens of conversations, growing more animated as alcohol slid down throats, pushed the music to the background. It was post-disco and Prince was playing. The lyrics set the stage for why everyone was there—"Delirious, I get delirious..." Cigarette smoke swirled up from the bar, hovering over the din of conversation.

Without a word to each other, Carolyn and Sara started a game they played whenever they went out for a drink: they counted the length of time it took for a brother to approach them. This time they got to nine–one thousand. When a man finally did walk up to them, Carolyn raised her eyebrows as if to say, "Maybe we better think about a makeover or check the number on the scales." Nine–one thousand was too long for Carolyn to wait for attention.

"Good evening, ladies. Are you enjoying your Friday evening?" Sara immediately felt sorry for the brother. She always hoped they would avoid a lame introduction. Carolyn always teased her about expecting to hear the likes of James Baldwin or Ralph Ellison in a bar. But it was Carolyn who could be so cutting. And the brother wasn't half-bad, either. Nice chocolate brown, neatly cut hair, broad shoulders. But he was wearing Hush Puppies. Sara spoke first to protect him from Carolyn's sharp tongue.

"Well, I guess we hope to. And are you enjoying yourself?"

"I am now," he said.

That was too much for Carolyn, who thought, "Two strikes and you're out tonight." She turned her back on the dude. If Sara wanted to waste her time with a lame dork wearing Hush Puppies, that was up to her. He had actually walked over to talk to Carolyn, as did 80 percent of the guys who approached the two, but he didn't mind shifting his attention to Sara. The guy used Carolyn's back as an excuse to move in between the two friends.

"And what's your name, pretty lady?" he asked.

"Jane," Sara said. Her momentary maternal instinct to protect this guy was fading with her patience.

"Jane. That's a lovely name. Jane what?"

"Jane, to you." She hadn't decided to go there quite yet, but the words flew out of Sara's mouth before she knew it. She saw Carolyn shoulders shake a little as she suppressed a laugh.

"Jane Tooyu. That's lovely, too. Is that Asian or what?" That was too much for Sara.

"Do you mind, we're waiting for our big, football-playing husbands," Sara said, trying to end the torture.

"Oh, I'm sorry. Very sorry. I should have known two foxes like you weren't available." He walked over to the very next single woman sitting at the bar.

"Maybe we need to find a new watering hole," Carolyn said, turning back toward Sara, "Mrs. Tooyu."

Just then, Sara spotted two guys who ran with one of her ex-boyfriends. Well, ex-boyfriend was stretching it—ex–bed partner was more accurate. She quickly scanned the place to see if he was there, too. But they seemed to be a duo tonight. Either they had seen her and waited for her to see them or had noticed her at the same time. They headed her way.

Sara nudged Carolyn discreetly. "Mmmm," Carolyn said when she saw the two. Ahmed and Peter weren't what you'd call fine, exactly. Ahmed was the more handsome of the two—taller, with a nice build. Peter was shorter and muscular, moving toward chunky. They weren't fine, but they knew how to dress—finely textured shirts and tailored slacks. They were smooth.

"Mmmm," Carolyn repeated.

"I know them," Sara cautioned, "and as far as I know, they like white girls—young white girls."

"Well, maybe they have a taste for some chocolate and taffy tonight," Carolyn said.

Ahmed and Peter gave Sara a warm hug. "It's been a long time," Peter said, lingering in the hug a little longer than Sara had expected. The scent of his cologne drifted up from her chest into her nose. It was fresh and spicy. She liked it.

Sara introduced Carolyn, who held her hand out to shake Ahmed's hand. He took it and put his other hand over it, squeezing it gently. The evening had new promise.

"So what have you been up to since our paths last crossed?" Peter asked Sara. It was a straightforward question, but something about the way he said it made it deliciously suggestive. Sara imagined herself lying on her back at a cross-roads, naked, her legs open. The earth was soft and she could feel the sun on her crotch, the rays lapping at her vulva, warming her lips, and gently encouraging her legs to open. She thrust her hips up rhythmically, fucking the sun's warmth.

Whoa. Where in the world did that come from? Sara felt a slight twinge down below. A little wake-up call. Hello, I'm here. When was the last time you got some good loving? She looked at Peter and remembered when they had first met. It was at a house party. They had danced together for maybe three songs before she'd met his friend whom she later started dating—or fucking. Peter was a fun dancer and there had been a strong attraction between them. The idea had crossed her mind more than once: what if they had started seeing each other? Tonight wasn't the first time she'd wondered if he fucked like he danced.

The conversation moved easily among the four, and then between the two they recognized as couples, and back to the four. It wasn't the deepest discussion Sara had ever had, it wasn't Baldwin or Ellison, but it was pleasant, light and frothy like the ice-cream sodas she had recently discovered a taste for.

"Do you think Prince is gay?" Peter asked.

"I don't care," Carolyn jumped in. "He is a bad little somebody. If he's gay, he sure knows how to get a woman's juices flowing."

Sara looked at Carolyn's glass. That last comment approached the raunchy. There was no more Kir in her glass. Sara saw Ahmed motion to the bartender for another one.

"Oh, really," Ahmed said. "Would that be orange juice or apple?" They all laughed, but Sara thought she should redirect the conversation before Carolyn took herself farther down the road of raunch.

"It is interesting how he makes androgyny so appealing," she said.

Carolyn wrinkled her nose, thinking, "Now we're going to have a dissertation on androgyny." Sometimes Sara could mess up a dream that was just about to get wet.

"Androgyny turns you on?" Peter asked.

"Well, I mean I think he has that effect generally." Sara backed up a little in the face of Peter's directness. But she didn't want to sound like she was dodging his question, either. "Yes, I guess it does turn me on in some way," she said.

"What about it has that effect?" Peter pressed. He leaned in a tad closer to Sara and she got another whiff of his cologne.

"I don't know. I never thought about it. Let me think." Sara envisioned Prince with his eyes exotically lined in dark eyeliner, and the way he danced, kind of squirmy but with serious funk. She raised her eyebrows and smiled.

"A penny—or more—for your thoughts. What made you smile so yummily?" Peter asked.

"I was thinking of how Prince moves," Sara replied.

"You mean like this?" Peter did a perfect imitation of Prince. Sara realized it was that same quality that had attracted her to Peter's dancing. He had that androgynous hit himself.

"Say, you want to go someplace and dance later?" asked Ahmed.

"Sure. Let's do it and get the juices flowing," Carolyn said.

They decided to order one more round. Carolyn excused herself and got up to go to the bathroom. She gave Sara an intent look that said "Come with me."

"Oh, me too," Sara said. Carolyn wondered how Sara had managed to grow up Black and female and not realize that women always go to the bathroom together. Carolyn peed for a long time. Sara was already at the sink washing her hands when the toilet flushed.

"Well, I think I might do this guy," Carolyn said, still getting herself together in the stall.

"Oh, really. That's a shock," Sara said.

"Why so sarcastic, Sister Sara? Why not? The brother is smooth, nice-looking, and I'm assuming because you know him that he's not some kind of sadistic psycho. Besides, I'm horny as hell."

"He's not a psycho, at least not that I know of. But from what I do know about blood, a condom is definite requisite."

"Bien sur." Carolyn always used French phrases when she was tipsy. With her index and middle fingers, she flipped a telltale small, square package out of her handbag a little too hard. The condom pack flew into the sink.

"Are you sure you haven't had a little too much to drink?"

"No. And so what? What is 'a little too much to drink'?"

"Well, maybe that's why you're so anxious to drop your drawers."

Sara and Carolyn were standing right next to each other, but they didn't look at each other; they talked to their reflections in the mirror.

"And so what if I am? I wish you'd get off your mother-superior trip. Of course I want to fuck him because I'm a little tipsy. Why do you think I got a little tipsy?"

Sara knew she sometimes seemed square to her friend, but Carolyn's comment stung. Carolyn could see she'd been too sharp.

"Oh, come on, Auntie Harriet. You know that's why I keep you around. To control my wild ass. If it weren't for you, I might be swinging from a chandelier buck naked." Carolyn pulled her friend to her in a big hug. Sara accepted the apology. They retouched their lipstick and Carolyn put another layer of mascara on her long, sweeping lashes.

"They're probably talking about the same thing," Sara laughed.

"Probably," Carolyn agreed.

"So if you want to do Ahmed, what are Peter and I supposed to do?" Sara asked with exaggerated innocence.

Carolyn turned away from the mirror toward her friend. "Well, now, the way Mr. Androgynous was all up on your ass, you might just think of doing the same thing."

"What do you mean?"

"Girl, I saw that little routine. 'Do you think Prince is gay? Does androgyny turn you on?' I saw your little hiney squirming around on that barstool," Carolyn laughed. "If I didn't want to do Ahmed, I might be interested in a little Adventure in Androgyny my damn self. If you weren't interested, that is."

"Maybe next time," Sara said as she pushed open the bathroom door.

"So, did you two have a nice chat?" Peter asked. "Or exactly what is it you ladies do in the bathroom together for so long?" He widened his eyes.

"Nothing, talk, what do you mean?" Sara asked. She squeezed between him and the stool to sit down. He didn't move to give her any room and her right breast brushed against him.

"Mmmm," Peter said. "Can I come next time?" Obviously, the two guys had the same conversation and Peter was the one designated to push the topic—the designated dick, if you will. Sara liked it. It kept that little twinge going that had started with her sun-fucking fantasy. When was the last time she had gotten some good love? She let him lean into her body as she sat on the stool, his crotch pressing perceptibly against her. She could feel his dick thickening on her hip and she leaned in ever so slightly, putting more pressure on his dick. It responded accordingly. Her boldness almost made her giggle.

The foursome continued their conversation, moving ever so subtly against each other. Sara opened her legs a little and arched her back, pushing down so she could feel the wood of the barstool against her pussy. Whenever she adjusted her body or reached for her drink, she rubbed down into the stool. Her panties were getting moist. The fact that she had to curb her movements and rub only periodically made it that much hotter. Peter and Sara didn't look at each other while he fucked her hip and she fucked the stool.

Sara was completely absorbed in their little barstool dance. She didn't know what she was saying and she didn't know what anyone else was saying, either. She tried to fake participation in the conversation by occasionally saying "yes." But she had no idea what she was saying yes to. Carolyn and

Ahmed might have said, "Are you an ignorant slut?" and she would've given a little distracted smile and said, "Yes." She could tell Peter was amused by it all.

It was so delicious, she couldn't stand it. "Excuse me," she said, sliding off the stool to get another rub of the coochie and another push on his dick. She couldn't wait for any girlie bonding trip to the bathroom; she didn't even take her purse. She walked quickly to the bathroom and went into the last stall. She leaned into the corner, lifted her skirt, and pulled her panties up between her buttocks, and hard against her vulva. She began rubbing her pussy with one hand while tugging on her panties with the other. It didn't even take thirty seconds for her to come. She leaned against the wall and caught her breath, slowly pulling her panties out of her cracks. "Whew, that was good," she said out loud. She decided not to wipe herself; she wanted to sit in the come juice and let it ripen into a nice rich pussy funk that might get licked off later if things continued to progress. She flushed the toilet, smoothed her skirt, and walked back out to the bar.

"Everything come okay?" Peter asked as she climbed back on the stool. He leaned into her hip and his dick was thick and rock hard. She looked down and it was quite visible between his legs.

"Oh, yes, everything is so satisfying," she said. She picked up her drink and took a sip. It had gotten a little watery.

"Shall we order another round or head out to the dance floor?" asked Ahmed. Sara had almost forgotten about them.

"I'm ready to party," Carolyn said.

"Me, too," agreed Peter, looking at Sara and meaning something other than dancing.

They decided to skip the additional round. Peter suggested they ride as couples and Sara imagined herself driving with his hand in her lap, squeezing her vulva, rubbing, slipping his hand under her skirt and pushing his finger into her hole through her panties.

"Why don't we follow you two?" Carolyn said to Peter and Ahmed.

They left Sara's car in the parking lot and rode in Carolyn's car. "So what was going on on your side of the bar?" Carolyn asked before they even got out of the parking lot. "I could feel the heat and see the steam coming up from your seat. What was blood doing, fucking you with his eyes?"

Sara laughed. She had guessed it might be obvious how turned on she was.

"It's pretty hot. I don't know, something about the way he moves, even when he's just standing there, makes me squirm."

"Are you sure you never fucked him before?"

Sara nodded her head.

"Ever thought about it?"

"I guess I have in a vague, undefined sort of way."

"Hmmm. Interesting..." Carolyn looked sideways at her friend. "And the boy doesn't even speak Baldwin." They laughed.

Ahmed was driving. He pulled over to the curb and Carolyn followed suit. Ahmed got out of his car and approached Carolyn.

"You know, I need to make a quick stop off at my house. These shoes are killing my feet. You could meet us at the club, but I'm afraid you'd get swooped up before we could get there. How about following me while I stop off to make a quick change?"

Sara and Carolyn looked at each other. "Very smooth," Carolyn said. "Well, what do you think? You feel okay with that?"

"I know these guys well enough to know there's nothing to worry about. Although you do know they have no intention of going to the club."

"Yes, I do. But then maybe we don't either." Carolyn leaned her head out the window. "Okay, we're right behind you."

They got to Ahmed's house and he, of course, invited them in for a drink. And, of course, they accepted. After pouring their drinks, Ahmed went back in the bedroom to find his "dancing shoes." He came back out in his stocking feet.

"Those are your dancing shoes?" Carolyn laughed.

"No. I can't seem to find them." He sat down next to her on the couch. "Let me think a minute," he said slipping his feet under Carolyn's crossed ankles.

"That helps you think?" But Carolyn didn't move; his feet felt soft and warm in his socks. He snuggled them a little closer to her.

Peter and Sara sat across the room from each other. Facing him directly, she suddenly felt shy. Peter picked up the change in her attitude and tried to figure out how to change it back. His dick was throbbing nicely.

"Well, since my buddy can't seem to find his shoes, why don't we put on some music and dance here?" Peter suggested.

Carolyn and Sara hesitated, not wanting to give up the option of going to the club just yet.

"Maybe he'll remember where he put his shoes while we're dancing. What do you call that, physical memory?"

Ahmed put on Earth, Wind & Fire. At first they all danced separately. As Sara moved, she began to lose that wave of shyness. Peter's dancing rekindled her curiosity. The way the man moved made her want to grab his dick, put her pussy on top of it and slide up and down until they both came.

"Hmmm," she said.

"Hmmm, hmmm," Peter responded without missing a beat, as if he were right there in her thoughts, just about to come. After two or three songs, the music slowed down. Peter pulled Sara towards him and put her arms around him. She had been anticipating melting into him, their bodies finally able to move directly against each other without the awkward positioning at a barstool. No fantasy, as hot as it had been—

just their two warm and eager bodies pressing together. But something about the way he pulled her to him put her off, interrupting her thoughts about them grinding against each other to a delicious wet frenzy. She pulled back and looked around to see what Carolyn was doing. She and Ahmed were moving together smoothly and Sara couldn't see any light between them.

Peter tried to pull her in closer, which only made Sara pull back more noticeably. During the next song, also slow, she tried to recapture that juicy, slithery feeling that had been radiating from her pussy, but she couldn't seem to get a hold of it. Just when she thought she felt it beginning again inside her, it slipped away. She frowned slightly.

"Hey," Peter said, realizing they were getting nowhere with Sara freezing up on him, "I heard about this stretching-exercise game thing. You guys want to try it?"

Ahmed and Carolyn were swaying together perfectly, their frames and crotches fitting like pieces of a puzzle. So Ahmed was less than excited about Peter's proposal. He had figured that after a couple more slow drags, he and his new lady friend would retire to another room—maybe even the bedroom. But he and Peter had been chasing pussy together for a long time, and he knew from Peter's out-of-the-blue suggestion that his friend had run into a hitch.

Ahmed thought it was funny how these things happened. In the bar, he thought Miss Prim and Proper was going to pull up her skirt and fuck his partner right then and there. He visualized Sara unzipping Peter's pants, opening his belt buckle, pulling out his dick, leaning him back against the bar, climbing up on the stool, straddling him with her skirt pulled up around her waist, and slipping her juicy pussy down on top of Peter's hard dick while the rest of the people in the bar watched, cheering her on and toasting their wild, oblivious fucking. That would have made quite an interesting bar interlude. Ahmed made a mental note to keep the fantasy in mind for future exploits. His dick stiffened as he thought about the scene and Carolyn pressed even closer to it.

Ahmed had thought that Peter was going to get to the gold long before he was, but things had shifted—his lady was just about there while Peter's was moving toward the front door.

"A stretching game, huh? I guess I can think of some things I'd like to stretch," Ahmed said, slipping his hand down to cup Carolyn's pussy through her pants. "Whew, girl," he whispered in Carolyn's ear, "I think you burned my hand."

Carolyn responded by breathing into the side of his face. Ahmed didn't want to take a stretching break, but he was sure it wouldn't get in the way of what he and Carolyn both wanted. It would just delay things a little. Sara, on the other hand, was relieved Peter had proposed a change in activity. Maybe she could get over this little glitch.

"Okay," Peter said, "first take off your shoes and we'll sit on the floor in a square." Ahmed could almost hear his buddy's mind working to invent the game as he went along. They sat with their ankles crossed, knees out to the side. Peter arranged them so he and Sara were across from each other and Ahmed and Carolyn were across from each other, their crotches open to each other, Sara's panties visible under her skirt.

First, they bounced their knees toward the floor. The movement began to loosen Sara up. The ice pack that had formed down below was starting to melt. When the bottom of her pussy first touched the hardwood floor, she wriggled to press more of it down against the floor. Peter recognized the subtle movement of her hips from her little stool dance at the bar. The girl sure liked the feel of wood between her legs, he thought. And he had his own piece of wood he'd like to let her move around on. His plan was working— but then, he had never doubted his skills.

Carolyn was worried she might leave a wet spot on the floor, not to mention in the crotch of her pants. She and Ahmed watched each other as they bounced their knees and after a few minutes, Peter said he was going to help each of them straighten out their legs into a V shape. He started with Carolyn, touching her ankle, then moving his hand up her leg to her knee and back down to the ankle. He pulled her leg into a straight and more open position. Her leg was shapely and felt good in his hand. He sneaked a look at Ahmed for assurance that he wasn't crossing the line. Both Ahmed and Sara seemed enthralled by Peter's hand on Carolyn's leg. He moved to the other leg, letting his hand brush against Carolyn's crotch. It felt like the temperature went up about ten degrees, and Peter knew it was probably wet, too.

"Hmmm," he said, still sure he wasn't offending Ahmed or Sara, but instead bringing them along on his sensual trek.

Carolyn's eyes were closed and after Peter got her legs stretched and opened, he moved on to Ahmed. He touched his friend with the same gentleness. Sara was surprised by how aroused she was at the sight of Peter touching Carolyn and Ahmed. It didn't seem to matter that one was a heterosexual touch and the other just this side of homosexual. She remembered wondering in the past whether Ahmed and Peter might have had some physical attraction for each other.

Sara was aching for Peter to get around to her. She bounced her knees harder, pushing her pussy down to the floor. Peter took his sweet time. He could tell from the hush and the rising temperature in the room that his game was exercising his real target—their libidos. And though Ahmed had anticipated fucking Carolyn, he was now considering a very hot foursome. Peter finally got to Sara. He positioned himself in front of her and gently pushed her knees toward the floor.

"You have a good stretch," he said. He put his index finger at the center of her crotch and let it slip down under her. He could feel the contours of her pussy, her fat juicy vulva swelling through her panties. He let his finger stay there, pressing gently into the curves of giving flesh that was so hot it almost did burn his hand. He moved his finger upward through the space between her lips, which were about to burst out of her panties, and to the top of her clitoris. He barely touched it, then let his finger drag back down through that inviting opening.

Sara closed her eyes, her lips slightly parted. She had that watery feeling she always experienced when she moved toward orgasm. She pushed harder against his hand. With the movement of her hips, she guided his fingers over her clitoris and toward the opening of her pussy. He teased her a little, moving his fingers away. She grabbed his hand and pushed it even harder against her.

"Whoa, girl," he whispered. His breath was sweet and hot and his lips brushed her ear. He licked the inner curve of her ear while he ran his finger between the lips of her vulva. "You want me to fuck you right here?"

Sara could feel a groan building and had to work hard to suppress it. She wanted to shout "Yes," spread her legs, and let him enter her with everything—fingers, tongue, dick, toes. But this little game of him stroking her with their friends watching was so tantalizing and protracted. She inhaled; her breath caught noisily. Sara was sure the floor was wet beneath her.

At some point, Carolyn and Ahmed had gotten up and left the room, turned on by the sight of Peter practically finger-fucking Sara in front of them. It was too much—they needed a bed. They moved quietly, although Peter and Sara were so pre-occupied they wouldn't have noticed if the other two had exited on elephants.

Sara opened her eyes and saw that she and Peter were alone. She pushed her pussy into his hand more vigorously. He smiled.

"Feels like you might have a pretty hot fever down here," Peter said, picking up the pace of his stroking. "Maybe we should take your temperature; I've got a thermometer." Peter deftly pulled his dick out of his pants. It was hard and thick, chunky, just as Sara had envisioned. The shaft was deep brown, darker than the rest of him; the head was shiny, almost glowing, so tightly was the skin stretched over his aroused penis.

Sara tried to say something, but her mouth was so watery she couldn't form clear words. She had to suck in the saliva so it wouldn't drool down her chin.

"Ooh, I like that sound," Peter said, his hand working all the time. Fingers probing deeper into the space between her lips and pressing more firmly when he got to her clitoris. "I'd like to feel that sound on a different part of my body." With his other hand, he took her hand and put it on his dick. She could feel it throbbing.

Her eyes were closed and she let herself sink into the pleasure of his hand stroking her and the feel of his hard penis. Her breath steadily quickened and they both thought she was going to come right there in the middle of the living-room floor. Peter stroked, gradually increasing the pace like the expert he was at getting pussy wet and juicy and ready for a good fucking. Her panties were sopping wet and he slipped two fingers inside, pressing hard into her hole. He put his fingers in his mouth and sucked them. "Sweet honey pussy juice," he said. He slipped his wet fingers back under her panties and rubbed and probed. The feel of her pussy made him moan. He put the fingers of his other hand to her lips, then gently eased them into her salivating mouth.

"Ooh, good," she half-sighed, half-groaned. Sara rubbed her hand up and down his stiff, thick dick. It was rock hard and yet the skin was velvety soft and smooth. She was ready, Peter was sure. Ahmed and Carolyn had left the room, so he and Sara might as well fuck right there. He pulled his fingers out of her mouth and placed them on her shoulder, softly pushing to get her to lie on her back.

She could feel the beginnings of the same uneasiness she'd felt when he'd pulled her toward him as they were dancing. She was determined not to let it grow into something that would keep her from satisfying this hot, throbbing longing between her legs. Whatever it was about his little push that made her uncomfortable certainly didn't outweigh the way his fingers were making her feel, sliding in and out of her pussy, rhythmically and with steadily increasing pressure. She focused on his fingers. Her pussy was opening up and her hips pushed toward his hand in the same rhythm of his stroking. The twinge of uneasiness disappeared and she let herself lie back. He came with her, as if they were attached—and they were, by his stroking fingers—straddling her and letting his body cover hers. The weight of his body was pleasantly heavy.

"You like this hard body, girl?" he said as he pulled her panties down. She kicked them off her legs. "You want this dick inside you?"

He didn't wait for an answer. He kissed her on the mouth. He had been aching to plant his full lips on hers. She opened her mouth and he stuck his tongue in. It was hard and chunky like his dick and she accepted it greedily; a hot current shot down her throat to her pussy as his tongue in her mouth simulated what his dick was going to do.

"Ooh," she groaned.

They were both ready. More than ready. He hurriedly pulled his pants down and off, opened a condom package and expertly slid the condom onto his dick. He pushed her skirt up, stroking her pussy again and pushing her legs wider apart. This time she didn't feel any uneasiness and gaped her legs as wide as they would go as he replaced his fingers with his dick.

It was wider than her hole. He pushed it gently against her, pushing steadily as her pussy opened up more to accept the head, then the top of the shaft. That boy sure did know what he was doing. She pulled his hips toward her and pushed against him as she opened up to let more of his dick in.

"Ooh, good," he moaned. He opened his eyes and he saw she was watching him as they fucked. That made him even hotter. "Ooh, good pussy!" He was just about to come when he stopped himself. "I don't want to run off and leave you," he whispered. "Ladies first."

He kept his dick in her, but with great control stopped thrusting it in and out. His hard, still dick felt heavy inside her, giving her the sensation of being completely filled up. She could feel the orgasm beginning. He took the tip of his index finger and lightly brushed her stiff, protruding clitoris. She moved roughly against him, pushing her pussy onto his dick as the orgasm radiated from her crotch, moving like a wave that washed over her torso, down through her legs and out of her toes.

She moaned as the orgasm engulfed her. He began to thrust his dick in and out again and they rode through the end of her orgasm and the beginning of his. He stroked, the delicious tension building—and finally erupting.

His warm cum filled the tip of the condom. They stayed like that, his dick in her, frozen except for the occasional spasms of their post-orgasms. Like aftershocks, she thought, feeling completely satisfied.

Peter looked up and saw Ahmed and Carolyn in the door-way. He wondered how long they had been there. They had surely seen some part of their fucking. He didn't know how Sara would feel about it, but the idea that they had been watched made his dick stiffen again. Sara felt it.

"You want seconds?" she asked. This boy could not only fuck, he could keep on fucking.

"I sure do. But we've got company."

Sara turned her head and saw Ahmed and Carolyn. She felt embarrassed at first, but she was so satisfied that the feeling didn't last. Instead, she felt a twinge of excitement between her legs.

"Mmmmm," Ahmed said approvingly. He and Carolyn were apparently pleased and excited by what they saw, and were ready to get in on the action.

"I've got an idea," Peter said as he got up, expertly pulling the condom off his dick without spilling the contents. His dick was still partially erect. "Why don't all of us get out of these clunky clothes so we can be more comfortable?"

"Clunky clothes?" Carolyn asked. She couldn't keep her eyes off Peter's partially aroused dick. As she looked at it, it stiffened even more.

"Sure," Peter said, "we can strip down."

Carolyn could hardly keep herself from grabbing Peter's nice chunky dick. And knowing it was still warm from Sara's pussy made her want to hold it and stroke it that much more.

"I don't think so," Carolyn found herself saying, more to caution herself not to reach for Peter's dick than in response to what he had just said.

"What about you two putting on some teddies?" Ahmed suggested.

"Oh, you just happen to have some teddies?" Sara asked. She was sitting up, but left her skirt hiked up so her crotch was still visible.

"As a matter of fact," Ahmed said, "yes."

"Well, why don't you two put on the teddies," Sara said playfully.

"Why not? I've always thought I would look good in one of those," Peter said without skipping a beat. He and Ahmed turned and disappeared into a back room. Carolyn looked at Sara.

"Girl, that was seriously hot. That boy can fuck!" Sara said. It surprised her that she didn't feel any embarrassment knowing what Carolyn and Ahmed must have seen. In fact, the thought of them watching was sustaining her feeling of arousal.

"I saw. Are you up for this foursome thing that we seem to be moving toward?" Carolyn was definitely interested in jumping on Peter's dick, but she wanted to make sure her friend was comfortable with it.

"Maybe so," Sara said. "Why not? How was Ahmed? Does the boy know how to crunch the noonie?"

Before Carolyn could answer, they heard Peter and Ahmed returning. They looked up in anticipation, aroused by the possibility of fucking en quatre. Instead, they had to look away to keep from bursting out laughing.

"Clunky clothes?" Carolyn asked.

The two guys stood there in all their manliness, with their broad shoulders, muscular calves, and rusty knees. They were bursting the seams of the teddies, their dicks poking against the sheer material, making little tents in front of them. Ahmed had gone the full nine yards and wore a garter belt that matched his maroon teddy with lace trim around the leg openings. But the garter belt was too small and couldn't stretch enough to get over his calves. It was stuck in the middle of his legs, causing him to waddle like a duck when he tried to walk.

Sara began to snicker. She covered her mouth to try to control herself, but the snicker was fast becoming a chuckle. "You...you two, look..." Sara pointed first at Ahmed, then Peter. And then she lost it.

"What?" Peter asked, feigning offense, "You don't like this color on me?" Peter's teddy was lime green with a forest green bodice that didn't quite cover his massive hairy chest and erect nipples.

Carolyn was laughing just as hard as Sara was. They tried to control it, but then Peter said, "We could try stretching again."

"I think there's enough stretching going down already," Carolyn said, and the two women lost it completely. The more they laughed and the harder they laughed, the more Peter knew he had gone too far down the path of no return. There would be no more pussy tonight.

"How did I make such a major miscalculation?" Peter said to Ahmed. "Shit, not only did I blow the four-way, I won't even get a second round in Sara's sweet nookie pot."

The guys sat down on the floor and their balls fell out of the lacy leg holes of their teddies. Ahmed's fell out to the right, Peter's to the left. Carolyn and Sara took a look at the pitiful sight and their laughter became uncontrollable. Every time they looked at Peter in his green and Ahmed in his garter belt, they broke out in a fit of laughter more riotous than the last.

All these years later, Sara fingered the garter belt her friend had sent in the mail. She couldn't believe it had brought back such detailed memories, or that she'd forgotten that very hot and very funny night. Remembering the sight of those two in teddies, she laughed so hard she started crying. She used the garter belt to wipe the tears from her eyes.

Peter had indeed been right. The laughter ruled out any more sexual activity. The hot foursome evaporated in the women's irrepressible spasms of laughter. It had taken them close to an hour to stop laughing and crying and slobbering. When they got themselves together, they accepted Ahmed's offer of a cup of coffee before they gathered their purses and jackets. Ahmed gave Carolyn his garter belt as a souvenir and the women thanked their hosts and left.

"I know, man. I know." Peter said when the women had gone. He wouldn't even look at Ahmed, who was glaring at him.

"Teddies are permanently crossed off the list of get-in-their-panties routines," Ahmed said. "I mean, draw a picture of one, put a circle around that bad boy, and put a thick red line through it. As a matter of fact, put two thick lines through it!" He pulled off his teddy, tearing the lace. "That shit was all up in the crack of my ass and squeezing my balls. Man, I sure hope I didn't do any permanent damage."

When Carolyn and Sara got in the car they started to chuckle.

"Don't start again, girl. I've got to drive. Do you realize it's almost daylight?" Carolyn said.

"How time flies when you're with the Teddy Boys," Sara said, leaning over and holding her stomach as she collapsed into hysterical laughter all over again.

Bring On the Bombs:
A Historical Interview

Nikki Giovanni

"It was tense all over the South all the time and not just because of the *Brown* decision. It was tense well before that. Things like the Depression didn't help but, my goodness, things like freeing the slaves didn't help either." She laughed. "I guess if we could have gotten rid of the tension, put it to a vote, don't you know, a lot of folk might, just might, have said Well, Let's Go Back to Slavery and Everyone Will Be Happy." It was a throaty laugh, deep like a kitten purring. "But you know those folk who live with us who really hate us would never be satisfied. Not 'til the last one is dead or so totally humiliated. What did Mrs. Parks up in Montgomery say? Why Are You All Always Pushing Us Around? Now that's my kind of woman. It just had to stop!

"We were running the newspaper. That's all he had ever really wanted. He loved journalism. We pushed real hard when the New Orleans bus boycott happened. We really tried to get the word out. Funny. Everyone remembers Montgomery but most folk have forgotten New Orleans. We always thought that without New Orleans, Montgomery would have been twice as hard. And, Honey, it was hard enough as it was.

"Course the main difference was King. Rosa Parks was the candle, was the light, don't you know, but King was the flame. Oh, that young man used to stop by our home to talk with L.C. We always presented him as the fine young savior that he was. Everybody talking about King was unsure and unworthy and all those terms people use when they are in the presence of greatness and don't know how to react. Hhhhpf! I never knew a man so comfortable in his skin. He knew exactly who he was and what he had to do. And was smart enough to let everybody think they were teaching him. He and I used to sit here some evenings waiting for L.C. and he would start in with questions so I knew he knew what had to happen. Martin, I would say, don't work me over. I know the drill. I've watched you. And he would just crack up. Lots of folk think he got it from Daddy King but if you ever saw Momma King work a room you'd know exactly where he got it from. We'd have a mint julep, which everybody knows isn't really a drink, and wait for L.C.

"We didn't travel much during those days. I'm partial to trains because I'm from a teeny tiny town and the train would go through in the morning and come back in the evening, that's the way I looked at it then. It was coming and going. I don't know where I thought the tracks ended but it was like this great big play toy rumbling through and all I could think is I want to be on it. After Momma was killed and Daddy left town, but you know, we never did see Daddy again and I always thought they were together somewhere. I would dream about them and they would be all dressed up and happy. They would be smiling at me telling me to be a good girl. I guess I always thought they were together. I would cry in my sleep sometimes but now I know what I thought is they were dead only when you're a little girl you don't know that so I just saw them together. The man who killed my mother lived in town. I used to see him when I went to the store. People would talk and nudge and whisper. I always stared at him. He drank a lot but lots of folk drink a lot, and they didn't kill my mother. She was pretty. I used to hear folk say he 'forced' her. It took me the longest to understand what that meant. The people who reared me were good people. They didn't want to talk about it much so I didn't talk about it. One day my father, my adopted father, took me for a walk and told me everything. We never talked about it again. What could anyone do? Momma was dead. The white boy did it. And that was that. I must have been twelve, thirteen years old. I know now he told me because I had become what is called 'a woman.' They wanted me to be careful. I wasn't the one who was not 'careful' but that's the way we looked at things then. What they wanted was for me to be ugly and to carry myself in an ugly way so that nobody would think of me as...Well, you know. So I tried all my life to be unattractive. Clean. Neat. But unattractive. Wouldn't you like a cup of coffee?"

The kitchen was not the kitchen of a woman who cooked. There were fresh cut flowers on the counter, a dishcloth with wonderful little birds on it, a rack for stacking washed dishes, an oval rag rug on the floor, a round mahogany hand-planed table with six chairs. "If this table could talk," she continued. "Oh, so many people passed through this kitchen, sitting at this table, discussing how we were going to change the country. Thurgood Marshall was a regular and you know, there was never a nicer fellow. No matter how bad things looked he could spin a story and have all of us laughing. Wily Blanton, too. Wily had that twang so white folks never knew they were talking to a colored man until they actually saw him. Wily was a total crack-up. But brilliant. Absolutely brilliant. Those men taught all of us how to get through tough times. Some music, some laughter...and well, some strategy, too.

"My father, my adopted father, died just before I finished high school. There was never any question of going to college anyway. L.C. used to come by the house to sell insurance. When things were going well he would take us all to the movies. But he would sit next to me. And hold my hand. I have an old friend who used to always say to me: if an older person wants a younger person, the younger person doesn't stand a chance. I never thought like that. I was thrilled back then. But maybe I didn't stand a chance. Kind of like old Uncle Ernie always putting his hands in the wrong place. Who could you tell? What kind of sense could you make of it? You just worked very very hard on never letting him get you alone. Of course, the grown-ups are so strange. Don't they notice anything? Don't they see how uncomfortable, no, *distressed,* you are? But they just drink and laugh and leave you out there by yourself to try to figure it out. L.C. wasn't like that so maybe that's why I trusted him. Anyway, after my father, my adopted father, died and I graduated from high school I married L.C. Seemed like those were my choices: marry L.C. or get murdered." That laugh again. "Well, maybe not exactly but women have really tough decisions to make. You know who I admire? Mrs. Parks. I guess the world admires Mrs. Parks, but the older she has gotten the more feminist she has become. She's one tough old bird. People were jealous and tried to act like she didn't know what she was doing but she damned well did. She knew ever since Emmet Till that somebody had to do something. Talk about a wake-up call. The horrible murder of Emmet Till rang a resounding bell to everybody. The *Brown* decision was in but the South was having none of it. As Roy Wilkins said It Was Because He Was a Boy. Those men murdered Till to show all the parents what they would do. But Till put some iron in our backbone. Everybody had to stand up. I'm not a mother, at least I didn't birth children, but can you imagine the pain of Till's mother to go reclaim the body and then open the casket?

Jet and *Ebony* ran the pictures, as did *The Afro-American* and *The Pittsburgh Courier.* So did we. We ran a special issue. So the tension was high and getting higher. Then came Rosa Parks and King and Montgomery.

"We really thought Little Rock was, well, different. There was talk but most people were for obeying the law. Ike wasn't much of a president no matter how you cut it and his remarks about the Supreme Court were regrettable but still nobody thought it would come to what it did. The school board reassigned the students; they went to register for Central High and we thought everything would go smoothly. There was an election going on but no one thought Faubus would have a chance. George Wallace down in Alabama had said when he lost his first election that he would never be 'out-niggered' again. Well, talk about 'out-niggering.' Faubus just stirred up the hate but he couldn't stir what wasn't in the pot. I have never understood the depth and breadth of white hatred. I'm glad I know it's not all of them. But something so crazy happens. All of a sudden normal-looking people start to spitting at you and tearing your clothes. Normal-looking people start to kicking children and pushing them down stairs. Normal-looking people are so incensed they are calling for blood. No one ever had to tell me what it was like that Friday on Gethsemane. Everyone was screaming for His blood except for a few of His friends. The crowd was so bad He told John to take His mother home. People were calling to release that thief Barabbas. But what did He do? What had He done? I always knew what it must have sounded like. The crazy screaming. The hatred. People haven't changed all that much, have they? The city started to go crazy. You could feel the tension. Still we thought everything would go smoothly. The police chief was suppose to take care of things. We did hear rumors that people were coming from Mississippi, Louisiana, Memphis but we weren't expecting what we got. Mobs hanging around. The national press, thank God, started to report so we weren't alone but it was frightening. Reverend Taylor was the NAACP head but he was an elderly gentleman and he thought with the coming troubles we had better get a younger person in the leadership position. He proposed that I run—which I did, and I was elected. Now, I was the one to find a way.

"We started meeting with The Children to work out how this would go. I didn't want them caught off guard if I could help it. Of course, everyone knew who I was so there were phone threats and all. Still, we weren't too worried. Well, the night before The Children were to go to Central, the mob was getting frantic. You could feel it all over the city. Faubus called out the National Guard and forbade The Children from entering the school. We didn't realize until too late that Elizabeth Eckford who didn't have a phone had not been notified. That's the picture you always see of the girl trying to walk away with the mob screaming for her blood. God, that was awful. But we pulled through. Still the calls, hanging me in effigy, all the threats were really bothersome. We had our guns, we're country people so we know how to hunt, and our neighbors had their guns watching the block for us. We had this really beautiful picture window in the living room. I think a lot of houses had them, that 1950s-type GI housing. I used to love to turn off the lights and watch the stars through that window. Well, when the trouble started we pulled the curtains. But the second or third night we heard the glass break and a brick came sailing through. I was coming down the stairs when it happened but I wasn't struck. The glass was flying and L.C. came running in. I think I may have been cut a little but mostly my nerves were frayed. There were too many people in my house, there was too much hatred in my hometown, there was too little possibility of help coming. Well, just everything came together or I guess I should say fell apart. You asked me what was the most thrilling part of my participation in history? I can tell you it wasn't just The Children integrating Central and being safe. Ernest's graduation was mighty satisfying. No, it wasn't the awards we all received. If a low spot was losing the paper, a high spot was reopening it even though it took ten years to do it. It wasn't even the President's Medal which never in my wildest dreams had I thought I would receive. No.

"I started crying and it just escalated on me. I went, I guess, from tears to sobs to some kind of hysteria. I just couldn't control myself. L.C. put his arm around me and started for the back of the house. That bathroom there, in fact. Reverend Taylor was at the table with some people and Chris said to him: Daisy and I Need to Be Alone. I learned later Reverend Taylor just pulled his chair up to the bathroom door with his rifle across his lap. Chris pulled me into the bathroom and looked around for the candle. We kept candles in each room because of the storms. I always like good-smelling candles in the bathroom so he lit them and the scent of lavender flowed. Chris put the stopper in the tub and ran a hot bath. He started unbuttoning my blouse and he was talking real soft, like you do to a crying baby or a wounded animal. He was kissing me and whispering to me while he took my bra off. I had chill bumps but I knew I wasn't cold. He was brushing my hair back while unzipping my skirt. He kept rubbing my back and my skirt fell on the floor. He pulled my half-slip over my head taking my arms way up high. His mouth was all over me, his fingers were playing inside my ears, then his nails were softly grating down my back. I tried to push his arm and found my fingers in his mouth so I traced his teeth then his lips then his chin. He pushed my panties aside and took control. I don't know if I screamed or dreamed that I did but it seem as if he lifted me by my middle and put me in the tub. He pulled my panties off as he settle me in the tub. We had the old-fashioned claw-footed tub so I was mostly sitting while he took the Sweetheart soap and rubbed under my arms, over my breasts, on my legs, and then he put it right next to me. I got to tell you my teeth were rattling. Chris was my husband and I liked him and didn't mind doing my wifely duty but this was something else again. He practically made me sit on that soap and I broke out in a sweat. I never thought it would have been possible to want anyone as much as I wanted him right then. I was trying to pull him into the water but he just kept going over and at me with his mouth and the soap and the water. His shirt and tie were dripping and his pants were wet. I stood up because I couldn't take it anymore and when I stood he took both his hands and opened me and whipped my middle with his tongue. I felt like I was on a boat riding a fifty-foot wave. I tried to step out of the tub but I needed him to put his hands in my front and back to keep me steady I was trembling so much. As he lifted me down my hands were on his zipper. I didn't want to wait to get his pants down I needed him then. I don't know how we ended up in the chair but Chris was sitting there and I was on top of him. Lord, what we must have sounded like. When he didn't have any more to give I unbuttoned his pants and thanked him properly. We both just trembled and trembled. You know, Chris was much older than I was and always very solicitous of me. But this time he owned me, possessed me, made me feel the power of his love without apology. He took my head in his hands and guided me back to him. He let me know how much it meant to him. We moved back to the floor where he took his pants off but the shirt and tie were too wet and too much trouble. He lifted my legs over his shoulders and all I could say was Yes. Chris said, Daisy. I Want You to Remember This When the Mob Hollers Tomorrow. I Want You to Remember to Come Back Home to Me.

"They said I was brave; that I was cool, calm, and collected. What I was was happy in the contentment of being totally needed. I used to go to that front window, which we never repaired until the troubles were over, pull back the curtain, and holler: Bring On the Bombs, Crackers! Bring On the Bombs."

Talkin' Smack
Blanche Richardson

Oh, hi! What are you doing here? I thought it was Jamal. Were you supposed to meet him here? No? Well, come on in; you can keep me company until he gets here. Let me take your coat. Mmm. I love the way leather smells, don't you? Nice slacks. You been working out? That silk shirt kinda clings to your body. I like it. Very smooth. Chocolate is definitely your color, my brotha! Why don't you have a seat—on the sofa. I sprayed the chairs with fabric freshener, so they might still be a little damp.

Why, thank you! I can't believe you remembered my birthday. How sweet. Listen, we're all going to the club tonight. I was gonna call and see if you and your lady wanted to come, but...well...I didn't know if...you know. Anyway, Lynn and Kathy are gonna be there. Even LaRhonda. And you know LaRhonda don't hardly ever get out! Gina and Alicia are up from LA and Raymond is coming, too. David's got that kick-ass commute all week, but I think Lena can get him to show. Roxanne? Now, you know it ain't a party without Roxanne and her cans of "act right!"

Anyway, we're gon' get our groove on, you hear me! So, why don't you come with us? After we've danced our butts off, everyone's coming back here for breakfast. I made fried chicken, homemade mashed potatoes and my special gravy, butter beans...You can smell it? That's the cornbread; it's still in the oven. I was gonna wait and make it later when we got back, but Jamal was taking so long, I needed something to do. You didn't know I could cook? Shoot. Not only can I cook, but dessert is my specialty! Tonight? Well, tonight, Monsieur, I am serving my world-famous gel rouge avec zee peachéz du cannes à la mode. Oui, oui. All us great chefs parlez vous français. You had four years of French in college? You never told me that. It must have been that *white* French. See, I'm talkin' Black French. You want the translation? Red Jell-O. With canned peaches. And Cool Whip on top. Don't laugh; I'll have you know this is considered a delicacy where I come from. Oh, so whatchu tryin' to say? I'm ghetto? Damn skippy! In fact, I'm gonna put my birthday candles in the Jell-O. I've been waiting for this night. My birthday hardly ever falls on a weekend, so I figured I'd throw myself a party. C'mon and go with us. Please? Well, will you at least think about it? Good enough.

Listen, can I get you something to drink? I'm having a Rémy. Double Rémy Martin straight up with a water back. I love saying that! I heard one of my mother's friends say it at my cousin Avé's wedding reception. I thought it sounded *so* sophisticated. I practiced saying it in the bathroom mirror over and over until I got the look down. Then on my twenty-first birthday, a bunch of us drove to Reno. I walked up to the bar at the first casino we went in, leaned in, inhaled on a cigarette, and said—in a low, kinda sexy voice—"I'll have a Rémy. Straight up. With a water back." Then I let the smoke drift up out of my mouth. I thought I was *too* grown. Of course, I choked on the cigarette and threw up that first Rémy. You go ahead and laugh, but I *know* I was cool.

I usually don't drink anything stronger than wine, but I need a little something to mellow me out. I don't want to be in a bad mood when Jamal *finally* gets his ass here. And I definitely don't want to have an attitude on my birthday. I mean he's your homie; you introduced us. You and me? We've been friends since what? Junior high? How come you didn't tell me your boy was so irresponsible? Lately I don't know if he's gonna be fifteen minutes late or a day and fifteen minutes late. And tonight, he hasn't even bothered to make his getting-to-be-like-clockwork hey-baby-something-came-up call.

Now don't look like that. You don't *have* to say anything; it's all over that handsome face. I can tell you're not feelin' me. I know when you introduced me to Jamal that you and me were starting to—you know—become more than friends. And I thought we had potential. I did. But you know how it goes. Fate stepped in and Jamal and I hooked up. But we're still friends. Right? No hard feelings? I guess you wouldn't be here otherwise. I like that about you. You just took it in stride, moved on the down the road and hooked up with Miss Thang.

Well, I'm gonna get a refill. A little one this time. I hear you. I'm gonna chill. But he's already two hours late and I hate to wait. A beer? Sure. I got plenty of beer. Jamal's favorite. Go ahead. Make yourself comfortable. Put on some sounds. Be right back. I've got to check on the cornbread, too.

Here's your beer. Use the coaster please. Thank you. You like this CD? I bought it yesterday. Thought it would make good lovemakin' music. There's that look again. Sorry, didn't mean to get personal on you. So where *is* Lynette tonight? I thought the two of you were inseparable. Last time I saw you, she was all up on you. You still with her? No? That's good. I never really liked her vibe. I mean, she's cute and everything. And the girl can dress. But she acts like she all that. Running her fingers through that fake white-girl hair every ten seconds and shit. Rolling her eyes at all the sistahs. Well, ain't nobody "all that" in my book. At least not behind no tight body and a weave. Know what I mean?

You got the time? Wait a minute! Hold up there, brotha. Let me see that watch. Ooo wee! Business must be very, very good! And it's not too flashy either. I didn't even notice it at first. You got good taste. I like that. Nice hands, too. I wonder where the hell Jamal is. I'm cool. But, damn! He could at least call. Page me or something. You know?

So tell me, why'd you dump Lynette? Oh, sorry. *She* dumped *you*? That chick is crazy. What happened? If you don't mind me getting all up in your bizness. You lying! Another guy? That's cold. You didn't have any idea? None? I can always tell when *I'm* about to get kicked to the curb. You have to pay attention to the little things, you know. A look, a tone of voice, a smell even. But you didn't pick up on any clues, huh? Blindsided your ass, huh? That's cold. Playing you like that. I mean, if you want to get with someone, tell me! Don't play me until you got a foot in somebody else's door. It ain't that serious, ya know? Plus, that shit is stupid. You hurt someone when you don't have to. You lose a friend. You get a bad rep. I never want any negative-ass vibes out there about me. I try to be up front and honest, even if it's hard sometimes. I don't want nobody feeling like no fool behind something I did. That pisses people off. The truth is what goes around…that's right…comes right on back around. And that's real!

Yeah, that's cold. I'm sorry that happened to you. You're a nice guy. Respectful, ya know? A gentleman. You know what? That's your weakness. Yeah, now that I think about it, that probably *is* it. You're *too* nice. Too much like right. You got yourself a good education, your own business, you love your momma, you're sensitive and responsible, you read books *and* you're intelligent. Damn, my brotha! I don't know how you *ever* get women!

'Course, on the plus side, you drive a phat car, your condo is screamin', you got plenty of cash...well, credit cards, but that still counts, and you're fine. No doubt about that. But there's no flash and cash about you. Know what I mean? No? I bet you've never even been arrested, have you? No. Flashy jewelry? No. Five children by three different women? No. See? That's what I'm talkin' about. C'mon, you don't even wear an earring. Even Michael Jordan wears an earring. Oh! My bad! Didn't even notice. Come closer. Lemme see. Is that a diamond? Mmm, you smell good. It's pretty small. But it's nice. I like it. There may be hope for you after all.

But clearly, my brotha, you are *in* this ghetto, but not *of* this ghetto. I mean where's the adventure, the thrill? Where's the danger? The excitement? The risky behavior? I'm too young to hook up permanently with someone who's already a grown-up. My grandmother would love you. She always gives me a hard time about who I'm dating, says I don't respect myself. The last guy I took over to her house, she called a bum to his face. She will *never* meet Jamal, know what I mean? I'm still tryin' to find myself. I don't really know *what* I want out of life. Not yet. And there you are—years into your thing, already. It's scary, like premature aging. Know what I mean?

Now don't get me wrong. Jamal's smart, too, but he's using his smarts to get over. Over on women, over on his friends, over on life. Or so he thinks. He's nothing more than a damn hustler. We both know that, but he's *so* charming. And he can be very sweet when he wants to. I'm not gonna lie; if Jamal told me to jump off a bridge, I might not do it, but I'd damn sure think about it if he was smiling when he asked. He's almost *too* good-looking and he always manages to say the right thing at the right time. I wind up forgiving him for every wrong thing he does to me. Now, he's got pleasing a woman down to a science—*when* he shows up. But I know Jamal's a "bad boy." A snake, actually. And he's unpredictable. I never know what he's gonna do. *Why* is that so damn attractive? That little voice in my head is screaming: "Don't do it! Get away from that man! Run! Run! He's a snake!" And you know what I do? I say, oh yeah, *that's* the man for me. Ain't about *nothing*! Exactly what I'm lookin' for. Total opposite of everything my common sense dictates, 180 degrees from what I know is good for me. I cannot resist. I *have* to have him!

I don't *know* why. Do *you*? I mean, was it like that for you with Lynette? She pumped you up, huh? Made you think you were the *man*. And the sex was wild, huh? I figured as much. So, you know who it was? The guy? I understand if you don't want to tell me…I mean…What is *wrong* with me? Sorry. I'm talking too much. I know it. Let me shut up. Let's change the subject.

Oh, thank you. Red is my favorite color. I think it accents what you used to call my "Hershey brown" color. You don't think it's too tight, do you? I got it especially for Jamal. He likes to see me in stuff like this. Shows off my figure, he says. Makes me look sexy. Hey! Where'd you hear that? That's what my daddy used to say when I was a little girl. "Girl, you've got legs all the way up to here!" Used to crack me up. You been staring at my cleavage since you been here. It's too low-cut, isn't it? Too much of my stuff showing, huh? Go on, now. Tell the truth and shame the devil. It's distracting? What do you mean, "distracting?" I *know* you're a man, so what's your point? Like magnets, huh? So have you heard anything I've said all evening? Or have you been too magnetized? You heard everything, huh? Right. Repeat something. Anything. Tell me something you heard me say tonight while you were hypnotized by my breasts. Go ahead. I'm waiting. Get outta here! You *know* you wrong. I did *not* call Lynette a tramp-ho-bitch! You're so funny. And, no. I am not glad that you find an "old girl" like me still attractive.

What time you got, now? Shit! We should be shakin' our asses on the dance floor right now. It's my damn birthday! Everybody's gon' be wondering what happened to me. I know one thing, it's time to get this slow-ass music off of here. I want to hear some party music. You want to dance? Don't worry about Jamal. He wouldn't even notice. I guess he's pretty sure about how I feel about him. Sometimes I wish that he was a little jealous, but he could care less if I flirt, or dance with every man at the club. Besides, he's usually so busy checkin' his pager or on his cell phone...shit, it would serve him right to walk in all late and find me having a good time without him. But, frankly? It wouldn't bother him at all. You like Latin, right? Santana is the man. I have almost everything he ever did, but I'm partial to the old stuff. Gimme your empty; you want another one? You put some Santana on and we'll dance. We can start the party right here!

Whoa! Guess I've had enough Rémy for a minute. Falling over my own two feet. Got my li'l buzz on. You like these shoes? You do? I had 'em dyed to match my dress. Jamal says he likes me in high heels. Says they show off my legs. Oh, you agree, do you? Well, thank you very much, but I'm gonna kick them off 'til we're ready to go. Nope. Never wear them. No pantyhose for the kid; they're too itchy. And besides, I think my legs look good once I lotion them down. You remember this ankle bracelet? I guess so! You gave it to me on our first date. That's right; I wouldn't accept it. Told you it was too personal a gift. I think it was right after my grandmother called my ex-boyfriend a bum and I was trying to do better. But you slipped it in my purse when I wasn't looking. That was the same night you introduced me to your boy. Remember? I found it about a week later, but by then Jamal and I were...well, you know. Be back in a second.

Here you go. Nice and cold. Wait! Don't sit down! Let's dance. C'mon now, I saw you swinging that tight butt with Lynette. Jamal didn't know I was watching your ass all night, he was so busy watching Lynette's skinny little no-dancing ass…Go on, Santana, with your bad self. Oye como va! Da *daa* da! That Lynette. She don't know a good thing when she got it. Shoot! If she had any sense, she'd woulda stayed just for the way these buns move! I *meant* when you're dancing, but I'm glad to hear it translates to the sheets! Ooo! Dip me again! I love a man who can dance, and you're a good dancer. Hey, did I know that before? I did? I told you so? Well, I was right! I like the way your hand feels, resting on my hip like this. Not nasty, like Jamal. He acts like we don't have a bed to go home to. You know? Like we had to get our groove on all up on the dance floor in front of everybody. I like to dance when I'm at the club. I like to make love in private. Jamal doesn't get it. What *is* that? A guy thing? No? Then what is it? Oh. A Jamal thing! I feel that!

Wait, wait! Stop twirling me, I'm getting dizzy. Did you hear something? No? I thought I heard a key in the door. Wishful thinking, I guess. Now what time is it? You know what we should do? We should go on down to the club ourselves. You and me. Jamal will know where I am if he gets here and I'm not home. If he gives a fuck. So what if Lynette is there? Screw Lynette! We can show that stiff-ass heifer how to truly get down. She can't dance worth shit. She too worried about being cute. She'd probably have a heart attack if she started sweatin' or danced the curl outta that weave, with her off-beat ass. She's the kind of woman who's too busy watching to see who's watching her. You know what I'm talking about; she was *your* woman. Sorry, I didn't mean to hurt your feelings. Sorry.

You all right? This is a slow song. You want to sit it out? Okay, but no dippin' and twirlin'. Let me put my head on your shoulder, I feel a little dizzy. Mmm, this is nice. You feel good. I like the way you move. I love this song, don't you? I wish some man would do to me what Santana does to his guitar. This does feel good, though, all pressed up on your nice hard body. You didn't have to move your hand back up. I like the way it feels. Put it back. Makes me feel sexy. You better watch out. It *is* my birthday and I *do* plan on celebrating—one way or the other. Ooo, I am getting a little hot. Good thing the music stopped. I *said*...the music *stopped*. I know. I was feelin' it, too.

Listen, why don't we wait a few more minutes, then we'll head on out. My friends are waiting for me and you know what? I'm thinking that maybe Jamal and me got our wires crossed. Maybe he thinks I was gonna meet him at the club, not here. It's probably a big misunderstanding. I'll bet you anything that that's what happened. I could kick myself! He's probably sitting at the club right now wondering where I am. Probably pissed off because *I'm* late. I don't know why I didn't think of that earlier. Duh! See that's why I don't drink. Five more minutes? Then, if he's not here, we'll head on out. Let me get my heels back on, and get my coat.

What time is it now? That's not what I asked you. You don't know whether Jamal is showin' up or not. Who asked you that? Not me. I only asked you for the time, *not* your opinion. If I wanted your damn opinion, I would have said, "What's your opinion?" But I only asked you for the damn time. I *got* a watch, you know. I got a clock in the bedroom *and* the kitchen. So if it's too much trouble for you to look at your damn wrist and tell me the time, I do have options! You can keep your damn opinions to your own damn self! And nobody asked you to put that depressing-ass Barry White CD on. I *told* you. I want to party, dammit!

I'm sorry. I didn't mean to snap at you like that. I apologize. It's just that, well...it's my birthday and I spent the whole day cleaning and cooking and now I'm all dressed up and ready to go and Jamal is either late or waiting for me at the club. And you and I both know that Jamal won't wait too long for anything or anybody. So, can you *please* get your coat on and let's get out of here. Naw, I ain't crying. You the one oughta be crying. I *got* my man. You the single one around this camp. Oops, must have a hole in my lip! Drippin' all down my chin. Damn! This shit is way too expensive to be spillin' and shit. I got to pee. Excuse me, please!

Okay, I'm ready. Do I look all right? You don't even have your coat on. You haven't even moved...What? C'mon, what is it? You know something I don't know, huh? Tell me. Go ahead. What's up? I can see it in the way you're not looking me in the eye—or the chest—anymore. It's Jamal, huh? He's not coming, is he? You know why, don't you? Where is he? Is he with another woman? Shit! I *knew* it! I knew something was up. Truth be told? I've suspected for some time that he was cheating on me. Yeah, so? Maybe I *like* being in denial. It's the *truth* that hurts. I got to sit down; move over.

I am so...so...so fucking...pissed off! At Jamal, of course! Who the hell else! Doggin' me out on my *birthday*. Now ain't this just some shit! I got to take some deep breaths. Iyanla Vanzant says take deep breaths so you can be in tune with the universe; so you can open yourself up for the truth. I hate this shit! Why me? And on my birthday. Surely it *must* be somebody else's turn by now. What am I doing wrong? I meet a nice guy like you, then turn around and go straight for the King of Bad Boy. I swear! I knew Jamal wasn't right when I first laid eyes on him. But I pretended I couldn't see; pretended I didn't hear that little voice. No. I had to go and fall for the same okey doke. He's no different than the last good-looking, sweet-talking asshole I thought I was in love with. I *knew* he was jive. Knew it! But I figured I'd be able to change him once he realized that I was the only woman for him. I figured I'd have it all, the best of both worlds. A good-looking, sweet-talking, and eventually—sensitive, responsible, monogamous man-for-life. You see? Thought I was gonna have my cake and eat it, too. He'd straighten up and see the light and we'd grow old and wealthy together. He'd treat me like the queen that I am. You're right, I guess. I'm pissed off at myself for being so damn stupid! What the fuck was I thinking? I *know* better. Son of a bitch! Shit, how could he do this to me? I'm walking around on Fantasy Island with my head in the clouds and he's standing at the dock, waiting for "de plane, de plane!"

Well, go on. Say it. I know you think I'm a fool. Yeah, right. Sure you don't. Is that why you came over? To see me make a fool out of myself? I hope you're happy? But I don't need a witness, thank you very much. Don't! Don't touch me! I don't need your sympathy. Save it for yourself. Yeah, you're damn right I'm pissed! He's not worth it? Oh? Is that what you said when you found out Lynette dumped *you?* No? Then what did you do?

You came over here? What in the hell for? What? You lying! She dumped you for *Jamal?* My Jamal? Oh this is too much for one little birthday girl to handle. So *how* do you know all this? You saw them? Where? You were at the club tonight? Well what were they doing? No they weren't! Not in front of my friends! Not on my birthday! Now ain't *that* a bitch.

Let's both take some deep breaths. I don't believe this happening. Breathe in. Now hold it. Breathe out. I mean, what in the hell...breathe in. Hold it. Breathe out. We've both got dogged. Breathe in. Hold it. We've been had, we've been hoodwinked, we've been led astray. We've been clowned—big time! We're losers, both of us. Oh, hell no, not tonight. Tonight, *they're* the losers. Yeah, they're the losers and we're the winners. Screw their sorry asses. Oh! I'm sorry...breathe out! Whew! You were starting to turn blue.

Well, that sure as hell blew *my* high. You know what we need? We need some weed. Me, either. I gave it up a long time ago, when people still rolled joints. But Jamal left half a blunt somewhere around here and I'm gonna smoke me some tonight. I don't want to be this clear. Not tonight. You down? Now where did I see that thang? Yeah, here it is, behind the Bible—figures. You got a match? Look in the drawer in the coffee table. There we go.

Mmm! This is some good shit. Here, you want some? Like learning to ride a bike, huh? You never forget how. 'Course, it looks like *somebody* forgot how to pass it! Thanks. I can feel it already. You? No, huh. Then what the hell are you laughing at? Yes, you are. Those dimples are a sure giveaway. You think this shit is funny, huh? Well I don't get the joke. We've been dumped. Both of us. I don't see anything funny about it. Stop it! It is *not* funny. You gon' make me start laughing and I don't wanna laugh. Stop. I'm tryin' to be pissed off. Shit! Okay, it's funny, but it's not *that* funny. You're doin' too much...fallin' all over...on the floor and shit. Whew! Shit, now I can't stop laughing...this shit *is* funny. It's actually pretty fucking hysterical! I mean...here I am talkin' all this shit...oh, my sides are hurting...tellin' you about checkin' for signs...and he's doggin' me out. Don't laugh with your silly self—he dogged you, too...That makes him a dog-ass motha-fucka—with his crooked-ass teeth...*you* know it's the truth...oh, my stomach...I can't even talk. No, don't! Don't pull me. Stop, I'm falling! Ow! My butt! You could have caught me...Oh, stop. Please! Stop. I'm gonna pee on myself...I can't get up...I can't stop...laughing. Oh, God, please don't let me pee on myself...I just cleaned this carpet. Oh...shit! Let me catch my breath. Whew! I haven't laughed this hard since...since Jamal's zipper got stuck! Came all over his self. I thought I was gonna die, I laughed so hard. What bright side? You see a bright side to this mess? Oh, now that *is* deep! He coulda been my baby daddy! You're right. This coulda been *a lot* worse!

Wait. Let's lay down here on the floor for a minute. Relax a second. You know, you'd think we'd be consoling each other, not laughing like we just hit the lotto. Guess it's the weed, huh? And why does Barry White sound better than he did a few minutes ago? I have to say something. I want to apologize. I've felt guilty ever since I dissed you for Jamal. I was wrong. I mean the way it went down wasn't right. I've tried to rationalize it away, but I know I was wrong. And I'm sorry. I'm sorry if I hurt you. I didn't mean to; I couldn't help myself, I guess. And you stayed my friend. I'm grateful for that. I know you came over here tonight to keep me from going to the club and getting my feelings hurt. I truly appreciate that. I do. How can I make it up to you?

You want to kiss and make up? You know what? I don't think I've ever seen you from this angle before, like we're lying in bed together. I love your dimples. How come I never noticed them before? You've got nice eyes, too. I always wanted thick long lashes like that. 'Preciate what's been said, but mine are fake. I'm glad you like them, though. You know what else? I never told you this before, but that one time we did kiss? Well, I swear to God! I dreamed about your juicy lips and that killer tongue all night! Yes, I did. Oh, so you remember that kiss, too? Shut up! I know that one little kiss didn't make you feel all that? Well, if you insist. I do pride myself on my kissin' skills. I love to kiss. To me, it's like the best part of foreplay, don't you think?...well, here *is* that. Is that still lit? Let me get another hit before it goes out. I mean, when a guy touches my breasts—whew!...this is some strong stuff...sucks on my nipples...damn! No wonder I gave it up...well it's like a direct hit to my stuff, you know? But it all starts with the kissing. I think the mouth is the most sensuous part of the body. Don't you? I like big juicy lips like yours. And a thick tongue.

A probing tongue. You know what? I have a philosophy. You want to hear it? Okay. This is it: as the tongue goes, so goes the dick. Deep, huh? No, well, yeah. The tongue and the dick can both go deep, but what I meant was that *I* was deep. You know, having a philosophy and all? Shut up! I'm watching those dimples; you're laughing at me again. Anyway, I like to tease a little first, maybe wet my lips, like this, brush 'em over his lips; feel him out. Then, when I'm ready, I start exploring. I run my tongue all over his lips before I separate them and make contact with his tongue. Slow, you know. I like to take my time, sort of get to know his mouth before I see how far I want to go. Once I feel him get him all hot, I pull my tongue out. I kiss his forehead, his eyes, lick his lips before I go back in. I press my mouth onto his mouth and let my tongue tango with his until we're both ready to move on. You know, his hand under my blouse, caressing my breasts. His lips lingering on my neck, then down to my nipples, kissing them through the fabric of my blouse. My fingers under his shirt, on *his* nipples, easing down his chest to those wiry hairs right below his navel...Damn; I'm trippin' hard!

So what do you think happened? How'd I wind up with the doggee and you with the dogette? I'm *much* too fine and too intelligent to be in this situation. There must be some mistake. I don't know what *your* problem is, but me...? Right. Okay. So you're an alien. Uh huh. And you're here on earth doing research? I can see that. So what kind of research are you doing? Maybe I can help you. A survey, huh. You have a questionnaire or something? Only one question? Let me have it. My most erotic experience? Hmm. I guess it would be when Jamal and me went to see this erotic foreign movie.

I had to *make* him go with me. I was so tired of the movies he picked. We either saw flicks full of stupid toilet jokes or those macho action movies where everything blows up, or crashes, or explodes, or some shit. All the Black people die in the first three minutes unless, of course, they're Wesley, Denzel, or Danny. Anyway, when we got back here I asked him if he wanted a beer—'cuz that's all he drinks, you know. That's why I have two cases in the hall closet and one in the fridge now. Anyway, I go, "Jamal, you want a beer?" and he goes, "how much beer do you have?" So, I go, "Baby, you know I've got all the beer you could ever want." And he goes, "how 'bout pussy? You got all the pussy I'll ever want?" And I go, "you know I do." So he goes, "get in the shower." I thought he meant we were going to take a bath together— you know what I'm sayin'. But he stopped me after I'd taken off my sweater and my slacks. "No," he goes. "Leave your panties on. And your bra." Then he walks out and I'm standing there shivering in the shower. Well, he comes back in with a case of beer! Can you believe that! Didn't say nothin', opens the first bottle and pours it over my head real slow. At first, I was trippin.' Beer drippin' all down my body. Foam settling in my hair, my eyelashes, making this fizzy sound, and running down over my shoulders. Jamal just stood there and watched. I was so cold; I had goose bumps all over. My nipples were already hard from the cold, but they got really hard from the warm foam. He told me not to move. Then he took off his clothes, except for his shorts. He gets in the shower and starts lickin' the beer off my face. My neck. He opens up another bottle and pours it inside my bra. Then he squeezes my breasts, making the foamy beer seep over the top of the cups like waterfalls. And he catches the beer in his mouth. He took the next bottle and asked me if I wanted a drink. I go, "yeah," and he goes, "sit down in the tub." So I sit down and he gets down with me. So now we're sitting face-to-face and he pours the beer inside his jockeys and tells me to suck the beer through the material. Then he pours a bottle into my panties and does the same to me. You know, I never liked beer. It always smelled stale to me. But now? I get hard looking at all those beer commercials during football games. Jamal and I have our own little halftime tradition now. Or we used to. I love your laugh. Makes me laugh, too. Give me another little hit. No. You inhale it then blow it in my mouth. That's it, like two hits in one, huh?

Guess what, ET? Your friend is getting really, *really* big. Look? Damn. That's pretty amazing. Here, turn this way. No, over this way. See what I mean? Look at it. Wow. Does laughing do that to all aliens? 'Cuz I know some *good* jokes. I wanna touch it. I can? I just wanna run my fingers over it—like this. Does that feel good? Can you take these off? C'mon. You been talkin' all that smack about my "magnets" and my red dress and my pretty legs. I want to see some of that alien stuff.

Ooo! Now that *is* impressive. Pull it all the way out. No, here. Let me do it. Mmm, very nice. Let me feel it. I'm just gonna use one finger. Hold still. I'm gonna be gentle. Lay back. There. That's it. Relax. I promise I won't hurt you. Here, suck on this—just...one...finger...at...a...time. Go on, suck it good. I'm just gonna stroke it up and down and over this ridge here and...Hey! Did you see that? It jumped! It likes me! Let me try that again—under here...and up here...around the top.

Guess what. I got a secret; I don't have any panties on. What do you mean it's not a secret? How did you know? Well what in the hell were you doing looking for a panty line? Freak! I knew there was something I liked about you. Why don't I rub on this and you can do some research up under this red dress you like so much. Ooo! You're quick. Went right to the gold! Slow your roll; let's take this nice and easy. Yeah, that's it. Much better. Nice. And easy. Hold on, I wanna taste it. Everything. I wanna taste all of you. And I want you to taste all of me.

You're hungry? I know, baby; I'm hungry for you, too. Fried chicken! You want fried chicken now? You mean *now?*

Well, if that's what you want. You're going to have to let go of
my breasts, unless you're coming with me. Gimme a hand up.
No, thank you, I can take care of the food, but you can get a
sheet or a towel or something out of the linen closet so we
don't mess up my floor. There's silverware, plates, and napkins already on the sideboard. And put on another CD, will
you? I'm gonna get the grub.

Help me! The chicken is sliding off the platter! You got it?
Thanks. Yeah, put it down on the sheet. We got your potatoes...and butter beans...and...here, take the cornbread.
Oops! I forgot the gravy. Hold up, be right back. Do *not* start
without me.

Here's the gravy, and I found some cranberry sauce from
Thanksgiving. Dang! I haven't had the munchies like this in
years! Where's the silverware? I thought you were gon' get the
plates. All we have here are the napkins. I thought you were
starving? How we gon' eat without the plates? Oh, really. And
why is that? Oh. So I'm gon' be your plate and you're gon' be
mine. Mmm hmm. I see. That how they do it where you come
from? You know, if you don't learn some earthly etiquette,
someone's gonna figure out that you're not from aroun' here,
my brotha. But I do *like* the way you aliens eat. Help me pull
this over my head. You want to put the mashed potatoes
here...and here? Two scoops; you *are* hungry. You want gravy
on that? I know the perfect spot to keep the buttered cornbread hot. Yes, that's it. Right there. And the butter beans?
Ooo, I like that...a trail up my thighs so you won't get lost
gettin' to the cranberry sauce. Now I'm going to hold this
juicy—well-seasoned, I might add—chicken thigh in my
mouth; I want you to eat it down to the bone. And when your
lips get to mine, I'll show you how we earthlings do it.

Then you can be *my* plate, okay? I just want gravy, lots of
savory gravy. A little dab here...and here. I love earlobes. A
drop in each dimple, in the hollow of your neck and, of

course, across those pretty full lips. I wanna suck gravy off this six-pack and dribble it all the way down here. I'm gonna lick and suck gravy off every knuckle of every finger. Pour some on these tasty inner thighs, first this side...then this side. And then, a little over these luscious delicacies here and lick it all off—gently of course. By then the entrée should be good and hot. I might just pig out on the entrée, put the whole thing in my mouth at once.

Yeah. I'm sure. Just gravy. 'Cuz. After we clean our plates, I want to have plenty of room for dessert.

Lust at First Sight
Private Joy

That's not a typo. I believe in love and all the promise that it brings, but, umm, this isn't about me falling in love. Been there, done that, and didn't bother to buy the T-shirt. Love is confusing and hurtful, and honestly, I'm too young to be sitting at home crying over why someone didn't call. Lust, on the other hand, is very straightforward. It lets you know up front that all you want is to see what the person in front of you looks like buck naked and sweaty. It makes you want to see how their face contorts in the throes of an orgasm you induced. Best of all, it makes you want to remember what they sounded like the minute they screamed out your name in a fit of passion.

That's what I was thinking that night at The Deep, a really cheesy club for the bisexual and lesbian women in the city. The people you met there weren't exactly funding Hallmark with their loving sentiments. It was a place to meet and see what body parts would fit where. If you got around to exchanging names, then you were ahead of the game and somewhat of a freak. These couplings were short-term and needed only for gratification. The club lent itself well to the clientele. It was dark and full of big plush sofas and chairs. The bar was sunken into the middle of the floor so that when you came back up from getting your drinks you were surrounded by the bounty of flesh on display. I'll admit that I had my share of liaisons from The Deep but I generally only went when my girlfriend, Nicole, wanted to go cruising.

That was the case the night I met them. They were clearly together. He was about six-foot even, well built with a nice butt and wavy black hair that was twisted. He had dark mocha brown skin that seemed very smooth and luscious from what I could see. He was dressed well, which meant he took care of himself, but he was just icing on the proverbial cake. She was amazing, even from across the room under the dim lights of The Deep. She couldn't have been more than five-foot-four-inches tall, but she was rocking some three-inch heels. Her skin was caramel colored and she had dyed her short, curly hair a deep shade of red mixed with brown. It was striking on her, especially when it curled close to her large almond-shaped eyes. That alone would have made me take a trip over to her to see if she was interested, but the breasts got me. She was about a 34D and since nipples are my favorite food I had to go introduce myself.

I had been dancing with Nicole while we both waited for whatever it was we were looking for when I saw her. Well, I didn't have a choice on that, actually. Nicole had been grinding her groin on my behind while I was moving to the music pulsating through the floor. I had closed my eyes and was just enjoying the dance when Nicole slid her hand up my leather halter-top and pinched my nipple. When my eyes jerked open, I saw the woman who made me wet from thirty paces. When I pulled away from Nicole, she leaned over and kissed me before whispering "happy hunting" in my ear. I told her "always" and went over to the couple I was planning to bed.

They were sitting close to the door—a clear sign that she hadn't been here beforeon a big purple love seat. He was glancing around the room at the barely dressed women enjoying each other's company. When I slid down next to him, I noticed a sizeable erection and knew that I hadn't made my trip in vain.

"Hello, my name's Kandi. Would you like a drink? To dance? Me naked between the two of you?"

He coughed for a second before glancing over at his girlfriend. "Dana, I think we found who we were looking for."

So Dana was the reason why my panties were heated, but until she confirmed her interest I wasn't sure I was going to be able to do anything about that. "Well, I know your girlfriend's name now. What is yours, kind sir?" I asked as I started rubbing my hand along the length of his shaft. God, it helped to be bi—twice the loving when I was interested in sharing. That's not often. I'm usually pretty selfish with my naked time, but that's because my appetite is so ridiculous. However, tonight I would have to be willing to share because I didn't think the owner of the dick I was holding was going anywhere without Dana.

He shifted in his seat, but I just readjusted my arm and kept stroking. "My name is Jeff. You already met Dana, but if you keep stroking on me like that, you are going to meet the anaconda sooner than you think."

I smiled across the table at Dana, who was sitting there as silently as she had been when I got there. I was thinking to myself why men always feel the need to name their equipment, but hey, maybe he'd live up to the billing. "So, Dana, what are you looking for tonight?"

She spoke up then, in the most annoying voice I've ever heard. "Well, I'm here to meet someone to have a threesome with. I told Jeff that I was curious about being with a woman so he brought me here. I have to admit I'm a little nervous about this, but you have the most beautiful breasts I have ever seen and I'd love to get to see them up close."

You have got to be kidding. She had to be one of the most sexually appealing women I had ever met and she sounded like she was on helium. I looked over at Jeff, who was getting larger in my hand by the moment. Partially from the caressing and partially at the thought of his girl with me no doubt. When I gave him a quick squeeze, his attention focused back on the conversation. "I've seen you in here before," he said as he readjusted himself on the love seat. He pulled Dana closer to him then. I guess to remind him who he came in with.

"Really? When was that?"

"My ex was bi. I think you turned her out one night because she was never the same after we came in here."

"So you were looking for me or for her?"

Dana perked up at that and Jeff sat there slightly uncomfortable. He calmed his deep baritone voice and said, "Neither. I just figured that Dana might see someone she'd like in here so I brought her."

He was lying. I remembered him and he remembered me. And I wasn't about to forget his last very freaky ex-girlfriend. Janet or something like that. Girl had a body that would not stop and a tongue to match. Umm, I wonder if I have her number somewhere, I thought. "Well, look, boys and girls, it's getting late. I'm getting horny and if you two don't want to play, I have to get back to the hunt."

They looked at each other and then stood up and started moving toward the door. I was about to spin around and leave when I felt Dana's hand on my shoulder. "You are coming, aren't you? I still want to see those breasts."

I flagged Nicole down, which was rather hard because she was in the process of getting fondled on the dance floor by some freaky twins. When they hit a good spot, her eyes popped open and she saw me. We signaled good-bye and then left each other to our individual pursuits.

When we got out to Jeff's SUV, I stopped Dana from getting in the front seat. I pulled her into the back with me and pulled down the straps on the black slip dress she was barely wearing. I pulled down the dress so that her breasts were free and then started my assault. My left hand found her right nipple and started tweaking it until I felt it harden. Then I leaned in to kiss her. It was a quick kiss, just to get her started, but when my lips touched hers she returned the kiss with more force than I gave her. Before long, we were French kissing in the backseat as my hands palmed her breasts and she played with my braids.

It was slightly difficult keeping my five-foot-seven-inch frame upright while priming her for later, but as if she were reading my mind, Dana reclined in the seat. She pulled me with her so that I was lying on top of her and kissing her like all hell. She pulled my hand from her breast and led it down to her nether regions. I always take a hint so I pulled her panties out of the way and let my fingers start playing on her clit. She moaned and the car swerved.

I stopped kissing Dana for a second and said, "Damn, don't kill us before we get home. Pay attention to the road and I'll make sure you don't miss out on a thing when we get there." Jeff turned back around and I focused on the half-naked body in front of me. My right hand began probing her wetness. She wasn't dripping, but she was ready for whatever we could think of that night. I leaned back over and started sucking her nipples, switching from one to the other as she gasped for air. If she was curious when she got to the club I was almost positive she was sure by now, but in order to cement my intentions, I removed my fingers from her moistness and started sucking them clean.

At this point I heard Jeff's pants unzip, and Dana's eyes widened in amazement. I knew what he was doing, but I wasn't sure what she was going to do next. I was pleasantly surprised, to say the least. She grabbed my hand and shoved it back into her pussy. She started grinding on my hand while she played with her breasts. She kicked one of her legs up on my shoulder so that I could get a better look at my hand playing hide-and-seek in her cavern. As Jeff raced closer to their apartment, Dana approached her first orgasm of the night. I was sure the backseat of the SUV was about to be drenched, but under the circumstances, I don't think anyone minded. Dana started moaning louder and riding my fingers harder. She was almost slamming onto them by the time she stopped and unleashed a small flood onto my palm and the seat. She stiffened up for a second and then relaxed herself. She still didn't move her leg, but she slowly removed my hand from its resting place and began licking off my fingers. That was more than intriguing, to say the least, and it must have caught Jeff's attention because the car started swerving again.

Dana chastised him this time. "Baby, calm down, we'll be home in five minutes and I'm sure that Kandi isn't going anywhere now. Are you?" she asked as she climbed into my lap and started kissing me. She wrapped her arms around my neck—at first I thought it was to get closer to me. Then I felt her untying the straps holding up my halter. As soon as she got it untied it fell down under the weight of the twins. I knew I should have been wearing a bra, but the strapless wasn't working in the tight leather top with the 42D's. She gasped again at the sight of my tits. She began rubbing her breasts against mine and grinding her pussy on my bare knee. She slid off my lap and between my legs. She sat up just enough so that she could taste my nipples. She licked them slowly at first, but as we both got more excited, she increased her pace. When I let out a moan, she giggled and then decided to focus her attention somewhere else.

She pushed my legs apart and pulled up my skirt, where she was greeted by my tiny black thong. She was about to move the panties to the side so she could get to my clit, but I told her, "Just pull them off." She slid them down quickly and began caressing my thighs. When she got back up to see my honey pot, she gasped again. "Oh, you shave!" she exclaimed as the car turned into a covered parking lot.

"Yes, I do, and you can get more familiar with her in a second."

She sat up and was preparing to fix her clothes when I stopped her. "It's almost two in the morning so I doubt there are very many people out. I didn't see any patrol cars when we pulled up so you won't be getting arrested for indecent exposure. And besides, I'd like to see how your breasts jiggle in the night air so let's both just go as we are." She looked unsure but Jeff agreed with me so we both got out of the backseat as we were. Jeff got in between us as we walked to the apartment.

He fumbled with the keys for a second, but when he saw us groping each other behind him he was able to unlock the door. He turned on lights as he moved around the apartment. Dana led me over to the couch and had me sit down in front of her. She walked over to the stereo and put on some slow-grind music. It sounded like R. Kelly, but there weren't any words so I couldn't be sure. She climbed onto the big wooden table in the center of the room—as she had apparently done many times before—and started stripping her remaining clothes to the beat of the music. As her hips started to move me into a sexual trance, I felt Jeff standing next to me.

"Do you mind if I sit here?"

"I'd be offended if you didn't," I said, patting a spot next to me on the sofa. We both turned our attention back to Dana, who was almost naked now. She was still in those heels, which was intriguing enough for me. Something about a woman in heels always makes me horny.

I walked over to her and sat down on the table facing Jeff. She looked confused for a second, but then Jeff spoke up. "She wants you to sit on her tongue."

"You *do* remember me, don't you?" I smiled at him as I reclined slightly on the table and rolled my head back, awaiting my present. She stood over my face and lowered her pussy so that it was touching my face. I reached out for her legs to brace her because I was starving at this point. My tongue made contact with her wetness and a shudder went through us both. I played around her opening for a while. I wouldn't kiss her clit or part her lips until I felt her rock back. I ran my tongue around and across her slit until her heel moved back toward the middle of the table and she sighed. It was then that I thrust my tongue inside her and began moving her hips so that she was bouncing on my tongue. I moved my hands so I could pull her legs toward my face when she pulled away. I knew she would, because they always do the first time they come on a woman's face. She tasted amazing. Girl had to have a sweet tooth because her nectar was practically like candy. She bounced harder and harder on my mouth as she got closer to her peak. Then it happened. She tried to stand up then and I pulled her back to my face. She tried to push my face away, but it was too late. She started shivering and then her orgasm flooded my mouth. She screamed out into the air and started to rotate her hips on my tongue as she came down from her peak.

She stood up and reached down for my face. She leaned over and kissed me then. "That was so damn good. I'm glad you came over and sat down with us." Every time she started talking, a nerve pinched in my body somewhere. That squeak was killing my buzz so I kissed her again. This time deeper, though, so that she was getting another good taste of herself. She wanted to return the favor, but Jeff had beat her to it. He pulled off my skirt while we were kissing and grabbed my hips to pull me closer to his mouth. His arms were supporting my hips and his tongue was dancing over my clit. I moaned loudly then and my head rocked back against the table. The man had skills. I have to give him that. He sucked my clit and inserted two fingers into my wetness. He let it go with a long suck and then licked around his fingers as he probed me.

Dana was watching Jeff closely as he attended to me. I didn't want her to feel left out so I had her kneel back over my head so that I could enjoy her pussy again. She was facing him and riding my tongue. We were one big orgasm waiting to happen. She was caressing my breasts and providing me with an ample supply of fluid to wet my tongue. I started bucking against Jeff's face as Dana started pinching my nipples and rocking hard back onto my tongue. I moaned into her pussy as she screamed out into the air and Jeff groaned as he tried to swallow the rush of my juices. After we all started breathing normally, we moved into the bedroom. I crawled in first and lay back in the bed. I was ready to watch the two of them go at it, but soon found that I was not to be left out of the festivities.

Dana climbed on top of me and we started kissing again. Her lips were almost as sweet as the ones I had just finished tasting. We were caressing one another and licking whatever available skin was near our mouths. When I opened my eyes, I looked up to see Jeff standing near the corner of the bed. Maybe I had shortchanged the man. He was mighty pretty standing there without a stitch of clothing on. His member was in his hand and it most definitely deserved that reptilian nickname. He had to be at least eleven inches long and about two and half inches thick. He had to be doing some major reconstruction when he got up in someone. My mind started twirling at the possibilities. I was so distracted thinking about the anaconda in Jeff's hands that I didn't notice Dana crawling between my thighs.

I felt her tongue though and it caused me to catch my breath. I swear she had to have a photographic memory cause she licked me in almost exactly the way in which I had serviced her. The only difference was her partner wasn't as shy as mine had been. I grabbed a handful of her hair and kept her face in my wetness as much I could. When her nose hit my clit I almost came, but when I felt her chin in my pussy, I couldn't hold back. My body rose off the bed and I started moaning every expletive I knew. When I rested back into the bed, Dana looked up at me and smiled. She was about to come up to kiss me again, but Jeff and the anaconda stopped her.

He snaked his dick inside her with one thrust. She screamed at the suddenness of the intrusion, but quickly returned his thrusts. I lay in front of them fingering my clit and pinching my nipples. I watched in amazement as Dana not only took his assault but also seemed to be relishing it. She was about to moan out into the air again when he grabbed her head and shoved it back into my pussy. She wrapped her hands around my legs for support and moved between us like a well-oiled machine. Each thrust he gave sent her tongue further inside of me and it sent all of us one step closer to being over the edge. We kept shoving and moaning and bucking against each other for almost half an hour before Dana finally couldn't keep up. She moved off to the side of me and that was my cue to do the one thing that I knew would put Dana to bed.

I pushed her up so she was on all fours and then climbed beneath her so that we were almost in a sixty-nine position. I moved my hand to block Dana's tongue and played with myself. She got the hint and went back to enjoying Jeff's organ. On the next in-stroke I started licking the area that joined them so that I was able to taste both of them at the same time. Dana lost it and started shaking uncontrollably. Jeff wasn't able to hold on after that either and they both had mind-numbing climaxes.

Dana climbed away from us both and lay on the side of the bed. It wasn't long before we both heard her breath deepen and a slight snore begin. Jeff and I climbed off the bed. We turned off the lights and closed the door behind us.

We waited until we were alone in the living room to begin talking again. "I don't know if I should feel jealous or not. I mean, I never got a chance to sample the anaconda, was it?" I asked sarcastically.

He sat on the wooden table on which Dana had done her striptease and started stroking himself. "You are welcome to the anaconda any time you want."

"Is that right?" I asked as I knelt in front of him and began kissing the still-wet tool.

"That's right," he replied as he grabbed a handful of my braids and pushed my mouth down around his dick. Never one to insult my host, I lavished attention on his member. It was rock-hard and ready to go in what seemed like seconds, but I wasn't done yet. I licked around down the base of his shaft and caressed his sac with my hand until he pushed me back onto the floor.

"I don't think the two of you have been properly introduced. Anaconda, this is Kandi. She's as sweet as her name. Kandi, this is the anaconda, and he wants to see you up close and personal." He grabbed my legs and placed them on his shoulders before he slowly inserted himself into me. I sank back onto him and lost myself in the sensation of being completely filled.

We moved together gently until he was completely ensconced inside me. I closed my eyes and let out a low moan, which was his key to increase the pace. Before I knew it, sweat was dripping from both our frenzied bodies. I climbed away from him as he began plunging deeper inside me. He let me get half a foot away and then stopped me. He groaned at me to turn over so I did and braced myself. He grabbed my hip with his left hand and guided his organ towards my opening. With one quick thrust he was all the way in and I understood why Dana had been smiling so much. He felt so good this way. My body had to readjust to his girth, but oh, it was lovely once it did. We were bucking against each other so hard and fast that I felt the carpet scraping my knees. Oh, what's a little carpet-burn in the pursuit of happiness? We moved harder and harder against each other until we were both on the verge of cracking the walls with our screaming. How Dana slept through that I'll never know—but I'm glad she did. When my legs gave out, we ended up grinding against each other on the floor until neither one of us could hold it any longer. We growled at each other as we climaxed. Neither of us moved for a few seconds. Then Jeff looked at his watch and pressed a few buttons before letting his arm rest at his side again.

"What are you doing?"

"Had to set my alarm so that we wouldn't sleep too long," he said as he rolled over onto his side, pulling me into him.

"Oh. That's a good idea because I need a nap right now. But I'd hate to leave in the morning without a goodbye kiss from the anaconda," I said, smiling at him and kissing his sweat-covered skin. "I am going to have to stop meeting your girlfriends this way."

He laughed at me as he nuzzled into my neck. "How else am I going to be able to get away with making love to the most amazing woman I know with my girlfriend's permission?"

"I see your point. But hey, don't get mad if this one leaves you too. I didn't intend on that whole Janet thing working out that way and you know I don't really want *them* most of the time. I really don't even want this one full-time. That voice would kill me. But hey, if I could keep her mouth busy, it might be worth it."

"Yeah, well, you don't worry about them. This is about you and me. I'll take you home when we wake up and then we can do one more spin on the Jeff-mobile."

We quit talking then and relaxed into the floor naked and still entwined. He took me home in the morning and we did things to one another I don't think they have names for yet.

I've been in lust with Jeff since I met him in a straight club several years ago. We tried dating but we both had monogamy issues. We broke up but kept seeing each other whenever the physical urge took over. If he was dating someone when I called, he'd start whispering to her about his secret unfulfilled fantasy to share her with another woman. We'd both end up at The Deep and then buck-naked several hours later. Most of the girls were enjoyable, to say the least, but the last few were what wet dreams were made of.

I figure sooner or later we'll get tired of all the games and just settle into middle age doing freaky things with one another. But hey, even if we don't, I have an amazing number of memories. And those videotapes. But that's a whole different story.

Courtship Rituals

Tananarive Due

Because he was so tall, Reid was the first person Martine spotted as she emerged from the plane's ramp at Miami International Airport: a lanky giant standing over the waiting knots of Cuban families and sun-reddened college kids on Christmas break. His grin was all teeth, boyish. He'd grown a goatee since she'd seen him last, and it suited his shoulder-length dreadlocks so well that his new look was a revelation. Goddamn him, she thought. Beautiful in yet another way.

"Oh, girl, I'm so glad to see you," Reid said in a breath, wrapping his arms around her as if he could meld the two of them together. Pressed tight to him, she could already feel his penis semi-rigid beneath his linen slacks, the irrepressible lump nesting against her lower stomach. A promise.

Reid was wearing the thin, crimson-colored turtleneck she'd sent him for Christmas, but the cologne she smelled at his collar was not from her. Without wanting to, she'd already noticed a dark-colored bruise at Reid's throat he'd tried to hide beneath the turtleneck, and her spirits ebbed. She'd hoped, this one year, he might not have other women at the house.

"Rough stuff?" she asked, breaking their unspoken rule.

Gently, half-scolding, he patted her shoulder. "The driver's waiting out front. I know you love stone crab, so I'll have some Monty's brought in. Hope you're hungry."

Of course he wouldn't answer her, and she was sorry she'd asked. She felt her jaw tightening, but she forced herself to let the tension go, something she was unable to do with the same grace and ease as she got older. Still, she wasn't about to let anything—or anyone—ruin her weekend. Her trip to Reid's winter house each January was a tradition, and she anticipated it the way a child pines for Christmas presents and sweet potato pie.

"I'm starved, baby," she said, glancing toward his face, away from the bruise.

Reid smiled at her like an angel. *That's my good girl* was written in his eyes.

• • •

Since college, Martine's plan for Reid had been this: At some undefined time in the future, they would give each other more than soul-filling words, dizzying creative bursts, and occasional sex during hurried, accidental encounters whenever they both happened to be in New York, or in LA, or like that one freakish sidewalk sighting in Minneapolis they still laughed about. (She'd been in town to interview for an arts grant; he'd been there for a meeting with Prince, back when he had changed his name). Eventually, she predicted, they would stand still for each other. She'd *known* this, so she hadn't felt anxious. They both had their lovers when they needed to be held, but that had nothing to do with *Them*. If an idea struck them, they called each other from their lovers' beds in the middle of the night. "Damn, you turn me on when you're so fucking brilliant. I won't be able to go back to sleep for thinking about you," he might say, or she might say, or perhaps they said it in unison. Reid was her soul-mate, after all, and in many ways he was as fine a soul-mate as she could have molded from her own rib and the earth's dust.

Reid worshiped her, almost literally. He never screened one of his films without shipping her a tape of the rough-cut first. Six years ago, indirectly, Martine had been responsible for the stink when he had refused to sign the studio's first choice for the lead in *Judas* because she had casually remarked to Reid how wooden the actor was. "You, Martine," Reid told her that night, "are the other half of my psyche. Without you, I'm naked and blind."

He seemed to truly believe this, and at times, so did she. She'd found that she enjoyed being worshiped, and that she had a worshipful streak of her own.

Her last two documentaries wouldn't even have made the art-house circuit if it hadn't been for Reid Samuel's name and connections. And *Sisterlove,* in which Reid had invested, had been picked up for cable release in the summer—also Reid's doing. The way Martine looked at it, theirs was a relationship of desperately trying to repay their mounting debts to each other. It had been that way since they first met at NYU film school, and nothing had changed in fifteen years.

Yet, everything had changed in fifteen years. That was the part Martine detested.

What Martine had not counted on, what had not gone according to her plans, was that Reid had become famous. Now, she wondered why she hadn't seen it coming all along.

He was half Trinidadian and half WASP, with a round-tipped nose and skin the color of creamy coffee, but he was the sort of black man whom white people did not consider black; distinctive enough to be exotic, yet viewed as essentially harmless except by the weak-minded, who were repelled by his rapier intellect and generous looks the way dogs glower at larger adversaries from a safe distance. Every time she accompanied Reid to one of his monotonous star-fucking parties, she noticed at least one tight-lipped person shrink away from him as though overwhelmed by the sheer magnitude of his presence. Most others—those who wanted to learn, those who wanted to jockey for positioning, those who wanted to warm themselves in his glow—valued even a smile or a quick word from Reid, and they were downright giddy if they found themselves in the midst of a conversation huddle Reid was conducting, where truth-telling alone made him a genius.

She still felt amazed when she watched Reid hold court, as he deftly sidestepped egos and kneaded the brightest minds into frenzies. His lovely, refined West Indian accent seduced all voices of dissent. "*Yes,*" one of Reid's observers was likely to cry, yanked out of a stupor brought on by boredom or an empty wine glass, as surely as if Reid had dropped to his knees and brought his moist, full lips to the stranger's crotch. She wasn't the only one who saw Reid exactly for who and what he was. He was greatness unfolding before their eyes.

So, she *had* expected Reid's fame, then, perhaps. Only she hadn't expected what it would bring out in him.

• • •

Once they arrived at Reid's waterfront Mediterranean-style house, Martine noticed strawberries waiting for them; the berries were fresh and damp, stacked in a lush pyramid in a shallow white china bowl in the most conspicuous spot in the foyer. Reid had always enjoyed living well in a way that had never mattered to her, probably because he'd grown up so poor. "Hey, nice touch! Does your housekeeper feed you berries while she fans you?" Martine teased as she reached toward the dish.

Reid didn't answer, his face suddenly grim as he moved the berries out of her reach. He didn't seem to have heard her joke.

His housekeeper, Lourdes, appeared in the blur of her ivory-colored uniform, taking the plate of fruit in a rushed, fluid motion. Reid leveled a severe gaze at Lourdes. "How the hell did these get in here?" Reid asked, his voice so low Martine almost couldn't hear.

"I don't know, sir. *Lo siento mucho.*"

"Martine almost ate one."

"I'm so sorry, sir. I am." Lourdes met Martine's eyes for a fleeting moment with a smile that was both a greeting and an apology, and then she hurried away.

Without a word, Martine waited for an explanation, but there was none. His gaze preoccupied, Reid let his hand find the small of her back as he led her east, toward the stairway.

"I think is time I give you a proper welcome, *oui?*" he said in a sing-song voice, a perfect imitation of his grandmother. He nudged her hip with his erection.

Martine liked the sound of that, but she was still bothered by his sudden mood shift. Reid's mother had cleaned houses herself, and Martine had never seen him snap at his staff. "You OK?"

Reid finally looked at her, and half his mouth drew upward into an unfinished smile. "Yeah, sorry. Things are on the crazy side right now. Lourdes is taking a leave after today. Maya is just too much for her to handle." He sounded tired.

Try as she might, Martine could not ignore the unfamiliar name. "Maya…?"

"You'll meet *her* in a bit," Reid said, his smile reaching a sweet perfection.

My God, Martine thought with alarm, this man is actually in love. Or he thinks he is. The two feelings, Martine knew, were wholly interchangeable. Her stomach felt stony, but she forced out a trite, breezy response: "Gee, Reid, why is it that the women in your life never get along?"

Reid only chuckled, offering nothing. She knew better, but she prayed that Maya was only Reid's new Rottweiler. That would be nice, for a change.

But Martine forgot that thought, and everything else, once they reached the guest room and she felt Reid's warm, wide tongue tunnel its way into her ear. As he gently pulled off her blouse and then her bra, Reid lapped at Martine's skin, setting small brush fires on her neck, her nipples, her navel. His movements were so lavish they almost seemed studied, but with a rhythm that was pure instinct. His tongue felt as broad as the palm of his hand, and it seemed to wrap itself around her. Her nipples were already as hard as raw peas, nearly aching from arousal, and they thrilled under Reid's vigorous, eager licking. He flicked, circled, and then sucked at her with his mouth and tongue in concert, pressing his torso against the ridge between her legs. Martine felt a tide of pleasure traveling from her breasts to her swelling clitoris, which was already anticipating the arrival of Reid's tongue. Reid's fingers made teasing butterfly motions against her pubic hair, and Martine squirmed. "Please," she whispered, already begging. "*Please*, Reid."

Smiling, Reid obliged her.

Reid was the first man who had ever performed oral arts on her, back when they were still in school, and he'd had the gift long before he'd had much practice. Many men had pleasured her with their tongues since—and some of them with true originality—but it was only when Martine was with Reid again that her body knew it was back at home. Coaxed by his tongue, something inside of her unlocked.

A dart here. A dart there. Unexpected plunges into her vagina, then a quick, delicious exploration deep between her buttocks. Suddenly, to Martine, everything between her legs collapsed into moisture, wetness, and each of Reid's rapid-fire motions became indistinguishable from the last. She felt herself quivering, vibrating. His tongue had taken her now. She was his instrument, and he had tuned her. He was making her sing.

Martine screamed so loudly that any passerby would have mistaken her cries for the last pleas of a woman certain to die.

• • •

The year *Judas* was released, soon after the film won all those Golden Globes and critics were slobbering all over Reid as if the Second Coming had arrived at last, he called her one night very late, in a hushed, reverent tone: "She's here."

"Who?"

"The Thai woman. Didn't I tell you?"

He had purchased a woman in Thailand. She was a prostitute he'd met on vacation in Bangkok, and he'd literally *bought* her from her pimp for twenty thousand dollars. Absurdly, the way a new parent would show off his child, he e-mailed Martine pictures of the plain, boyish-looking woman. She couldn't be older than twenty. She spoke very little English, he'd written—mostly dirty words. He was deliriously happy.

That was the first time he had ever made her truly angry. "Isn't that slavery, Reid?"

"Don't be ridiculous. She's a rich woman now," he said.

After that, he stopped calling Martine with news about the woman and the carnal talents she'd learned since her introduction to the pleasure business when she was fourteen. Soon after, when his prize had borne him two sons, it seemed she didn't want to be a whore anymore; she wanted to be a wife and mother. Reid admitted to Martine that his obedient little Thai woman had suddenly become liberated and had threatened to take his children back to Bangkok when he moved two of his girlfriends into the house. To appease her, Reid bought her and his sons a condo on South Beach, ten minutes away, and he set out in search of less mundane pursuits.

One of his new girlfriends, he said, had been born without legs. She threw temper tantrums if he didn't have sex with her three times a day, and the sex was amazing. He spoke in great detail about the benefits of the flexibility allowed by her missing limbs, but she had stopped listening by then, trying to blot out the image in her mind of Reid's muscled arms lifting a legless woman's torso up and down the length of his beautiful cock. *Her* beautiful cock.

No wonder the Thai woman moved the children out, Martine thought.

She learned to stop asking questions.

• • •

The table was draped in a white tablecloth beneath the orange glow of lawn torches at the bank where Reid's yard met the intercoastal waterway. Martine and Reid had been alone at the table for ten minutes, sharing a bottle of a sweet South African Riesling, when Maya appeared.

Martine had often read about people described as *elfin,* but she'd never met anyone who so literally fit the description until Maya slipped into her seat. She was not even five feet tall and must have had the bones of a sparrow to look so delicate. She wore tight-fitting jeans and a black nylon T-shirt that clung to her nearly nonexistent breasts. But she was too feminine, too lithe in both form and movement, to be called *boyish,* not like the Thai woman, Panida, had been. Especially now, with a smile on lips glowing with a deep, natural rose. Her skin was either deeply tanned or naturally honey-colored.

The woman was not beautiful, but she was certainly appealing, so Martine wondered what her imperfection was— unless, of course, Reid had finally found someone who attracted him on a basis higher than novelty. Reid clasped Martine's hand, stroking in a slow circle with his thumb, probably to help put her at ease.

"Did you enjoy the strawberries?" the woman asked Reid, ignoring Martine's presence at the table. Martine picked up a trace of an accent she couldn't identify.

Martine could see only Reid's profile, but his jaw was so rigid that it looked like a stone carving. He must be staring at this woman with a level of rage she had never seen in Reid. This pleased her, until she remembered the symbiotic relationship between fury and love.

"What are the rules, Maya?"

"I was just being nice, that's all. I missed you."

"Bullshit. What are the rules?"

"I swear, Reid, I just wanted to—"

"Oh, really?" Reid said. He moved a hidden hand from beneath the table, and Martine saw that he was holding the bowl of strawberries, like a misplaced movie prop. Two strawberries jumped from the plate when he dropped it to the table. "Why don't you have one, then?" Reid asked, his grin steel. "Please. Help yourself."

Maya's jaw shifted as though she were chewing gum, her smile gone. "I hate to ruin my appetite after what's-her-face went through so much trouble to get those crabs. Maybe later."

"You better remember the rules. Is that clear? Or next time, you *will* eat one."

Martine could feel heat rising inside Reid's palm; his anger radiated through his skin. Martine felt an impulse to pull her hand away, but she didn't. She sat in the line of the poisonous energy being stoked between Reid and this woman, as though it pierced through her. It left Martine a paralyzed, mute observer. And wholly invisible.

Maya had stabbed her salad with her fork. "All right already. I didn't do anything to the goddamn berries."

"Promise?" Reid asked her.

"Promise," she said.

With that, not breaking his gaze toward Maya, Reid fumbled for one of the plump strawberries and tossed it into his mouth. He began to chew.

Maya grinned. "You're a brave little SOB, too."

"That's what you love about me, my witch."

Jesus, what the hell was going on between these two? Martine shrank against the back of her chair. The interaction between Reid and Maya had shifted from anger to something very different, to a heavily charged magnetism that made her curse herself for coming out to Reid's to be a part of his freak show. A part of her was horrified.

Then, of course, there was the part of her that was thoroughly intrigued.

• • •

Martine felt movement in the bed, and it woke her up. Until now, she had assumed that Reid had fallen asleep too. She checked the clock on the nightstand, a ticking rosewood antique with glowing hands, and saw that two hours had passed since they'd come back to her room after dinner. She'd forgotten how calculated Reid could be, lulling her to sleep in his arms, then easing himself on to his next order of business. He was never finished, never ready to rest. He always had something else, or someone else, to attend to.

"Stay," she said.

He kissed her forehead, then stood up and wiggled into his boxers. "See you in the morning. Sleep as late as you want," he said.

"Jesus." She didn't hide her annoyance.

He paused, as if to ask her what was wrong. But since he already knew, the only thing left was an explanation. "Maya expects me."

Lucidity began to creep back into Martine's brain, now that the combined amnesia of lovemaking and the disorientation of sleep were wearing off. "Who *is* that woman? Tell me her story. I know you're dying to, since she's got you so whipped you can't even spend the night."

There was no light from the hallway, just moonlight from the window, so Martine could only see Reid's silhouette. He didn't answer, but she imagined he was smiling.

"And that whole crazy drama with the strawberries. What was that about, Reid?"

"We'll talk about it tomorrow. It's a very long story."

"Get out, then," Martine said, rolling away so that her back faced him. "If you're through fucking me and you can't at least be entertaining, then let me go back to sleep."

He left, his footsteps so soft that she didn't hear him leave. She knew she would not be able to sleep, at least not soon. The warm area between her thighs was still singing holy praises, but her conscience was flaying her. The middle of the night was always the worst time to be alone at Reid's. She could never avoid the question: *What the hell am I doing in this loony bin? Am I a visitor or a patient?* That was one reason she was always glad when Reid stayed the night: fewer questions to keep her awake in the dark.

At the precise moment Martine began to doze, she felt her floorboards shake after a hard thud from across the house. She sat straight up, her heart jumping, wondering if the sound and sensation had been real or part of a dream. She heard distant footsteps, walking hurriedly. And a muffled woman's voice. Another crash, but smaller and accompanied by the sound of shattering glass. It sounded like a lamp breaking.

Then, utter silence.

Martine's thoughts were frozen. She couldn't sort through her impulses. More out of fascination than fear, she was riveted to the spot.

This time she heard closer footsteps, approaching her room quickly from the hallway.

"Reid?" she tried to whisper, but her voice stayed locked in her throat.

As if in response, Reid's bare arm appeared in her doorway, reaching for the doorknob to her half-open door. Standing in the hall, he did not peek inside her room. In a swift, silent motion, he pulled her door closed. He was so deft, she barely heard it click.

• • •

"Maybe you could start with that old cliché, 'There are some things about me you don't know,' " Martine suggested as she and Reid navigated through the sidewalk full of pedestrians on Ocean Drive. It was a sea of firm, sculpted men's chests, ample bikini tops, and middle-aged South Americans and Europeans who understood the arresting power of color-coordination, fine shoes, and an unhurried walk. South Beach, Reid often said, was his favorite place in the world.

"To say that would be a lie, wouldn't it? You know all about me."

That was true. She'd been so amused the time she and Reid had both ended up in the audience at the NAACP Image Awards, when he'd been escorted by a six-foot blonde wearing a glittering dress so tight Martine was convinced it must be leaving skin indentations, and her friend Sheila, a music promoter, had leaned over to point them out: "Ain't that your boy over there? Where'd he find his date, on the corner? Why can't the brothers just leave these white women alone? I thought that status shit went out in the seventies."

Martine had agreed, all the while suppressing a laugh because she recognized the blonde as Gary Diamond, a transvestite who'd had a mad crush on Reid for years, and who managed to keep company with him because of his access to exotic delicacies of all varieties. Martine knew Reid never touched men, or he would have gladly told her all about it— but he was willing to flirt with *anyone* to find new novelties to add to his collection. Diamond's date with Reid to the Image Awards had been a reward, no doubt, for a suitable offering in return.

But explaining all that would have been a bit too deep to go into with Sheila that day. So Martine had said something appropriate like, "Well, you know how it is, that European standard of beauty," and giggled to herself through the rest of the ceremony, most particularly as Reid stood up to give his acceptance speech and Diamond stared at the stage with adoring eyes.

"Yes, I do know all about you, whether I like it or not," Martine answered him. "And evasiveness isn't usually your style."

He took a moment to answer. This time, his tone was less casual. "As long as you're sure you know why you're asking, Martine."

"Why would I be asking except out of idle curiosity?"

"Maybe you have a lust for pain. Or something else less idle."

"I think you have me mixed up with Maya."

"I could never confuse you with Maya. You're the blood in my veins."

Gee, thanks, she thought, but she didn't say it aloud. No matter how much she might crave it, she wasn't going to turn this into a fight. A fight might mean release. Freedom. Suddenly, her chest was in a knot. "Tell me about her," Martine said.

"Over coffee," he said, and extended his arm to indicate an empty sidewalk table at the News Cafe. She reminded herself that this might have been the exact table where Gianni Versace had had breakfast the morning he was gunned down while walking back toward his home down the street. That thought felt like an omen.

"She was brought to me in November. I can't say by whom. She's a fugitive," Reid said once their steaming *cafes con leche* had arrived.

"You're harboring a fugitive?"

Again, a hint of a smile playing at his lips, self-satisfaction aching to burst out. "I wouldn't say harboring, exactly. Her room has bars and a padlock. I'm more like a caretaker."

"You mean a prison guard."

"Oh, she doesn't want to go anywhere. She's very happy with me."

"She didn't sound too happy last night," Martine said. Fugitive or no fugitive, she couldn't ignore the possibility that Reid was physically abusing this little speck of a woman. Was that his game now? And, if so, what was he turning into?

"You're so quick to judge. I'm disappointed," Reid said, pretending to pout. Gazing at his slightly puckered lips, Martine despised how his expression endeared him to her even though she knew it was pure artifice. She ignored an urge to rub his knee under the table. Or, better yet, to raise her bare foot to his crotch.

"What's she wanted for?"

Reid's gaze became intense. This, apparently, was the part he was particularly proud of. "She's a Black Widow. She's wanted in three states. She's killed four lovers, maybe five."

"You're joking."

"Not at all. She poisoned three of them. And one, she choked to death with—"

"So that's what that whole fuss was about at dinner? You thought she was trying to poison you?"

"It wouldn't be the first time. I had to have my stomach pumped before she'd been here a week. She put something in the milk." He said this, it seemed to her, with something like pride.

That was extreme, even for Reid. Now that she thought about it, she remembered he'd made a quick trip to the hospital last fall for what he'd explained was a stomach virus. She'd hardly given it any thought at all, since Reid had sounded so lively on the telephone.

"Let me understand this: you're carrying on an affair with someone who hates you."

"You're oversimplifying. She has urges to kill me sometimes, yes, but she doesn't hate me. She didn't kill those other men out of hatred. It's hard to explain, actually."

"I don't care about her psychological profile, Reid. But I have to admit, I'm very concerned about *yours.*" Suddenly, as she'd felt the day he called about the Thai prostitute, she felt that Reid had become a virtual stranger.

He waved his hand with dismissal. "Don't worry. I know it can't go on forever. But the delicacy of the situation fascinates me. And the sex is inspired. Not like it is with you—"

Martine barked an empty, sarcastic laugh. "Oh, Reid, please."

"No, I'm being sincere. She doesn't touch my core like you do. She's not in my bloodstream. How can I describe it? She's more like a bag of potato chips I can't stop munching on. Sooner or later, you feel sick and you stop eating, that's all."

"Either that or you get killed."

Reid sighed. "What can I say, Martine? I'm a daredevil. I keep expecting all my brazen risks to get me into horrible trouble one day, but instead they've won me an obscene bank account and a feast of female company. The only drawback seems to be that I can't have you. But there's a catch-22, you see. With you, I mean."

"And what's that?"

"You're always waiting, my queen." He shrugged, and she wanted to hit him, an impulse that had been foreign to her until today. Martine wondered if it had taken him a long time to glean that particular bit of insight, or if he'd known it all along.

"You *think* I'm waiting," she said coldly.

"Well, unfortunately for us," he said, "there's no difference between truth and perception."

Martine realized, with calm certainty instead of anger or grief, that this would be her last winter trip to Reid's house. Role-playing exercises became invalid as soon as someone broke character and pointed out all the make-believe. She just wished she'd done it first, not Reid. She wished she had noticed how far from her he'd strayed while he was right under her nose. Was he purposely trying to chase her away? If he was, he'd created yet another masterpiece in Maya.

"This thing you're doing with Maya, this game, is insane. I don't know where you got this woman or why you have her, but it's dangerous. And it's insane. You know that, but I have to say it."

For the first time, he averted his eyes. "I'm sure it looks that way."

"That's just the first thing. The second thing is, I'm not going to stay. You must think I'm crazy, too, if you expect me to spend another night—"

Suddenly, he took her hand and squeezed it warmly. "Martine, I promise you, last night was a fluke. Lourdes wasn't watching her properly, which gave her access to the kitchen while I was gone, and then that commotion you heard later—"

"I don't want to know." As if she were a third-grader, she wanted to cover her ears.

"Just listen to me. I usually keep her very secure. She just had an episode, and it surprised me. But I'll be much more careful. You can't think I would ever place you in danger. Besides, no matter how crazy this may sound to you, it's not you she's after. She has no interest in you. And a pickaxe in the middle of the night is much too crude for her."

"Are you listening to yourself, Reid? I hope so."

"OK, yes, she fascinates me. I'm sorry. I would send her away if I could, since she bothers you so much, but I can't arrange that on such short notice. I don't want this to intrude on our time, Martine. You know how I look forward to this weekend all year, having you to myself. I pushed back my shoot in Morocco for this! We have so many more interesting things to talk about. You see now why I didn't want to tell you? You're so intent on taking a position."

"Taking a *position?*"

"Why start casting judgment now? That's all I'm saying to you. Is this honestly so outside your expectations of me? Why pretend it is? You know who I am. Sweetheart, I can't bear to sit here fighting like an old married couple. It makes me want to cry when we argue."

His hand, as it clasped hers, felt like it was pulsing with every word. She honestly thought she was feeling his heartbeat until she realized her wrist and arm were radiating from his touch.

She had no choice. She sobbed. Her chest was breaking open.

"Shit," Reid said. He looked genuinely stunned. Even when Martine's father had died two years before, she had not cried in front of him. The notion that she never cried was one of the fantasies that she enjoyed perpetuating about herself. Reid glanced around uncomfortably, as though other diners would consider her tears some indictment upon him. Furtively, he motioned to their passing waiter to bring the check.

He stared at her mournfully, his eyes threatening their own tears. "Did I do this to you, Martine? You're my life, and I've hurt you, haven't I?"

She shook her head. "I've done this to me," she whispered from the thick wall of her throat. More than anything, she just wanted to be held. And when they got back to Reid's house, she decided, she would allow him to hold her.

Because, after all, they both knew that was why she was here.

● ● ●

Reid gave her a joint to help her put everything in perspective, and even though Martine hadn't smoked in years because dope made her lethargic for days afterward, she sat in his library and smoked the entire joint like a cigarette, skimming through Wole Soyinka's *Death and the King's Horseman* and thinking she understood it all at last. Sometimes the king has to commit suicide because ritual demands it, she thought, just like in the play. A king's gotta do what a king's gotta do. She felt like she'd gained enough perspective to last a year.

And when Reid came behind her, kneading her shoulders and asking if she'd care to join him and Maya in the pool, she couldn't think of one reason why not.

The sky had gone dark while she wasn't paying attention, and it was cooler outside than it had been the night before. Not New York by a long shot, but there was definitely a bite in the air. Bright lights illuminated the pool from under the water, and the rest of the patio was black. Martine tipped across the smooth, glistening pebbles of Reid's patio tiles, enjoying the prickly sensation against her bare soles. When she noticed that Reid and Maya were naked, floating serenely with their arms resting against the pool's edge, she climbed unselfconsciously out of her one-piece suit and tested the water. Yep, the heat was on. A heated pool in Miami had seemed almost beyond extravagance to her when Reid first had it built, but she was grateful now.

This is going to be a good night, she decided.

With a light streaming right beside Maya's body, Martine could see that the areolas centered on her tiny breasts were a dark brown, nearly as dark as her own. She could also see a dime-sized birthmark near her navel.

"Where are you from?" Martine asked her.

"Half of me's from Brazil, half from Lebanon. But I've lived between Georgia, Michigan, and California my whole life. Take your pick," she said. She paused, as if to say *You through with your questions now?* Then, she went on blandly, as if continuing an earlier conversation: "I think most movies are just dumb. The people are so fake."

Despite her mellow mood, her body melting in the warm pool, Martine didn't feel inclined to try to explain to a serial killer how script deadlines and sophomoric formulas had made characters virtually inconsequential in Hollywood. Let Reid defend his own, she thought.

"Martine would agree with you on that," Reid said.

"Like cute, happy little dreams," Martine said with a yawn. She enjoyed the familiarity of this debate with Reid, which reminded her of college. Even then, measuring herself against Reid had provided her a sense of conviction. "*Judas* was an important film, Reid. You proved you could do it, and then you went back to helping people sleep."

"I never saw *Judas*. I'm not really into the Bible and all that," Maya said. "But I know what you're saying, Martine, because I didn't like that big movie Reid put out last year at all. I just thought it was silly. Sorry."

"See that? You may be the only two people left who don't tell me only what I want to hear," Reid said, staring at Martine with such heavy-lidded eyes that she knew he was wishing he could broach the question of a threesome. He would never dare ask her, of course, but Martine wondered if this was the one time she might consent. They were all within a couple feet of each other, close enough to touch. The water lapping just below Martine's chin was lulling her to a place where no questions need be asked, and no answers were required.

"You must be broke as hell, huh?" Maya said to Martine.

Martine smiled ruefully, closing her eyes. "Something like that."

"Reid is a millionaire. He doesn't even pay attention to how much money he's got, 'cuz he's got so much of it. And people come here and kiss his ass all the time. The actors who are supposed to be so hot themselves are the worst ones. I've seen them."

"Me, too," Martine said. She liked Maya's candor, and she felt the sudden hope that everything Reid had told her about Maya that day was complete horseshit. "Is any of it true?

"Is what true, babe?" Reid asked, invisible behind her eyelids.

"I'm talking to Maya. Is it true what Reid said you did?"

Martine heard a playful slap and splash in the water. "How come you had to go and shoot off your mouth?"

"So is it true or isn't it?" Martine said.

Maya paused. "What did you say I did?"

"He said you killed four men."

Maya's voice grew slightly husky, sounding almost too big for her frame. "Well, then, he's a damn liar. It was five. He knows it was five."

Martine lay very still in the water, waiting to feel something. Instead, she wished she had her 16mm camera with her, that she was capturing the night on film. She couldn't pretend she was still an observer, though; she had become one of her subjects.

"Why did you do it?" she asked. "Why do you kill men?"

"It's just beyond my control," Maya said, sounding bored. "There are no...what's that word, Reid? That pretty one you use all the time?"

"Epiphanies," he said.

"Yeah, no epiphanies. I do it because I feel like I have to. I guess love has to hurt, that's all. Better them than me. But I'm going to stop, though."

"Now who's lying?" Reid said.

This time it was Maya's turn to laugh, a very merry and girlish sound. After a short silence she said, "What are you gonna do with your money, Reid? Put me in your will."

"You a crazy woman, girl, if you t'ink I'm going to do something fool-fool like dat."

"Who are you giving it to, then? Martine?"

Suddenly, Martine opened her eyes. She wanted to see Reid's face when he answered. He was gazing at her, smiling. "Should I do that, Martine? Should I give you my money?"

"Keep your money," Martine said. "You can't buy what you want from me."

"Why you gon' buy de cow fo', you get de milk fo' free?" Reid said, and this time it was Martine who gave his shoulder a slap. Afterward, Reid's voice grew reflective. "No, my money goes to my perfect little precious boys. Life will be good to them."

There was silence again. Whether it was because of the pot or the warm water, or both, Martine felt her spirit floating inside herself, untroubled. Reid, seeing her thoughts, reached over to stroke her chin with the ball of his thumb. His eyes sank into hers. *Those* eyes she knew like her own. They were not the eyes of a stranger.

"I love it here," Maya said, her voice sounding far away, a pattering. "This is the best home I've ever had. Have I told you that before, Reid?"

"To you, any home is the best you've ever had," Reid said, still gazing at Martine. She saw the silent, private plea to her in his face.

"No, I mean it this time. This one is the best," Maya went on.

"Me, too," Martine said. Relieved, Reid swallowed her with his gentle mouth.

It took Martine some time to realize that the fingers plying her nipples beneath the water were not Reid's. Maya's fingertips squeezed harder than Reid's, to the brink of pain, but Martine discovered that she didn't mind. Somehow, that seemed just right.

Maya's tongue and fingers were the instruments of a poetess, Martine decided. Martine had never been touched by a woman this way, had never been curious about it, but Maya's mastery made her a being beyond gender. She did not kiss Martine, offering only touch, not intimacy, which was fine. While Maya made Martine squirm and cry out from the most unexpected motions—a palm pressing against Maya's submerged belly while a wiggling finger gently penetrated her vagina, or the sensation of a tongue teasing at her clitoris beneath the warm water, making flesh and fluid nearly one and the same—Reid kissed her with his healing lips, whispering vows that were even more satisfying to Martine than the unseen hands squeezing and caressing her nakedness, washing her.

Four hands, each of them with its own mind. One voice in her ear, the voice she heard in her dreams.

• • •

"You okay in there?" Reid asked, knocking gently on her doorjamb. She hadn't seen him standing there watching her. He was shirtless, wearing nearly translucent white drawstring pants, with a small white hand towel draped across his shoulders. He was still lovely to her, but that was all. Tonight, she didn't long for Reid's presence in the bed beside her.

"Should I be?"

"Yes," he said.

"Fine. Then I'm okay," she said, and smiled.

Martine heard a sharp clink of metal, then Maya stuck her head in the doorway, more than a foot lower than Reid's. "Hey, there," Maya said, grinning mischievously. "Reid's getting me a late-night cup of tea. Want anything?" Martine was not even surprised to see that Maya's tiny wrists were bound in front of her in thick iron handcuffs that shone in the light in a way that made Martine think they must be very cold.

"Do you wear those all night?" Martine asked.

"Only if I don't want to be put in my room. Reid lets me sleep in his bed with these."

"Where'd you get those, Reid?"

"Lincoln Road Mall," Reid said. "I'll take you sometime."

"No thanks," Martine said, smiling. "They don't have my size."

Reid winked at her. "Precisely. I'm the one who's shackled where you're concerned, not vice-versa. Good night."

"Good night, you two," Martine said to them. "Be good."

She watched them walk away, Maya shuffling because her ankles were bound, Reid tenderly holding her elbow, helping her keep her balance. Something about the image struck Martine as profoundly moving. She was more tired than she could remember being in a long time, but she didn't reach up to turn off her bedside lamp right away. She wanted to wait for the sound of metal dragging across the hallway tiles as Reid and Maya walked back past her room to where they would sleep. She wanted to see them together again.

Waiting, she fell asleep herself. Then, for no particular reason, she snapped to alertness with a gasp. She glanced at the clock and realized that twenty or twenty-five minutes had passed. Had Reid and Maya come back through the hall? She didn't think so. She was a light sleeper, and she would have heard them.

Somehow, she was certain that too much time had passed. She remembered she was still a little stoned, because her chest was constricting and suddenly she didn't seem to have any sensation in her fingertips or toes. It took her a long time to realize she was only afraid. Anxiety attacks were another problem she had with dope, she remembered.

Martine sat up, wrapping her kimono around her nakedness. She found her worn leather sandals and put them on; she never walked on floor tiles barefoot, a lesson from her mother. Men want dainty feet, her mother had told her. She'd heeded her mother's lessons, or most of them, and none of them had prepared her for Reid. What Reid wanted, apparently, was much more than dainty feet. There was no way her mother could have predicted that for Martine when she was a college student on spring break, when Reid came home with her and kept her family laughing with his funny stories and sly smiles. She and her mother could see some of who he would be, but not everything. They hadn't seen Maya.

Reid's house felt much larger and more foreign at night, when most of the lights were off. He only spent a few months a year here, so he'd never put up photographs or imposed much evidence of his own tastes, not like his house in LA. The blandness of the hallway seemed to stretch forever. But there, at the end of the hall, Martine could see the fluorescent light glaring from the kitchen, no doubt bouncing off the shiny floor, the white appliances, the white countertop. The light offended her eyes.

And she heard something, too. The sound of quiet weeping.

Martine never had to actually walk inside the kitchen. She only had to walk close enough to see Maya kneeling on the floor through the entryway, her handcuffed wrists held up so she could rub her face. Martine was close enough to see a single strawberry on the floor, nestled beside Maya's bare, grimy foot. Maya walked without shoes, Martine realized.

"You said you didn't do anything to the strawberries," Martine said. Her voice was gravel, as if she were asleep.

Startled, Maya looked up at her. Her tear-damp face was no longer brown, but bright red. She was a woman in agony, Martine realized, and in this way they were really no different.

"I didn't. Not all of them. Just...one. I couldn't...help..." She was sobbing, incomprehensible for a moment. "I thought he...threw them...out..."

"Is that what you really thought?"

Abruptly, Maya stopped sobbing. She gazed up at Martine as if she were noticing her for the first time and had somehow decided tears and explanations weren't necessary for her.

"Well, anyway," Maya said, drawing in a long, clogged sniff to clear out her nose, "I'm going to stop. I really am. Just like I said."

Without saying anything else, not realizing she was capable of making the decision to do anything, Martine turned around and began to walk toward the foyer, toward the waiting front door. She wasn't shuffling as Maya had been earlier. Her steps were steady and quick.

"Even if you call a doctor, it's too late!" Maya shrieked after her. "You hear me? It works real quick. I've done this lots of times before. Five times, not four! This makes six!"

The chain-lock on the front door always stuck because it had been splattered with thick paint some time ago, and Reid usually had to show Martine how to jostle the pin just right to free it, so she could get out of his house. But Reid wasn't here standing over her as he usually did; Reid was lying somewhere on the kitchen floor while a crazy woman cried over him.

And Martine was determined, more than she'd ever been about anything, that she was going to unlock the door and open it, even if her fingers got bloodied and it took all night.

Lifestyles

Aya de León

Three condoms sit in the bottom of my bag, ripening. One black, one white, one mint-flavored. Lifestyles.

"Hey, we're getting old in here," they whine. "Our biological clocks are ticking."

The black condom has a little red bow tie on the wrapper that says "Tuxedo," and has a superiority complex.

"Excuse me, Miss Thing. How did I end up down here in some nasty purse?"

"It's not a purse, it's a book bag."

"Whatever. Girl, you need to clean this mess out. Old scraps of tissue. Dust. Some kind of crumbs, and just general filthiness. Chile, don't you ever vacuum in here?"

"I'm really busy. It's not high on my priority list, okay?"

"Well, pencil in into your date book, girlfriend. This state of affairs is not acceptable. I am the high-end condom. A cut above. You need to keep me in a red silk box on the bedside table with some soft jazz in the background. Yeah."

"Sorry. I don't have those kind of accommodations."

"Well then, take me back to the basket at your job.

I must've gotten picked up by the wrong person, and some other second-rate condom is living out my destiny. This is a downright switched-at-birth tragedy."

"You know," I tell him, "the Yoruba say that we pick our destinies before birth."

"Don't give me none of that voodoo-hoodoo mumbo jumbo. Just take me back, okay?"

The white one says, "I don't think she's gonna go for that."

"Well, then could you at least clean up the bag?" the black one asks.

"I'll put it on my to-do list," I say.

"Like that's gonna help," the black one gripes.

The mint one pipes up: "Our best chance out of here is for her to use us."

"Oh, right," the white one says. "Getting laid is probably on her to-do list right *below* 'clean out the bag.' "

"The problem," the black one says, "is that Miss Honey is way too picky."

"Too picky?" I say. "These are dangerous times."

"Don't worry," the white one says, his voice thick with nonoxynol-9, "we'll protect you."

The mint one says, "What about that firefighter you dated back in December?"

"He never called back."

"Well, why don't you call *him?*"

"I did. He was a blocked artist."

"If you like artists so much, why don't you call that painter you dated a few months ago?" the black one says. "He was fine."

"Yeah," I agree, "but he left after a few dates to sleep with someone else."

"That's 'cause you wouldn't give it up."

"Oh, well," I say. "That shows he was only after one thing."

The mint one says, "He wasn't only after one thang. He was after a lot of thangs, sugar. But the sex thang was a really *important* thang."

I suspect she is right. But I don't want to give an inch on this. "Whatever," I say.

"She's impossible," the white one complains.

The black one says, "What about the brother who took you to dinner the other night?"

"Hold up," I say. "Get it right. We each paid for our own meal."

"Okay, have it your way," the black one says. "What about him?"

"He wasn't interested in my work or my writing. That's the main thing, here. I have a destiny to fulfill, and..."

"Our point exactly! We have destinies, too." The black one, the white one, and Ms. Mint were in agreement.

"Look," I said, "I can't just shackle myself to some guy who isn't about anything."

"Speaking of shackles," the mint one says, "I heard a story today about a ribbed condom at a sex club. You want to talk about action..."

"Hey!" I say. "Will you please keep it down in there. I'm trying to write."

"Just tryin' to inspire you," the mint one says in mock innocence.

"Save it," I tell them.

"That's the problem," the black one says.

"Okay, that's it!" I exclaim. "I can't concentrate at all." I take them to the bathroom and seal them in a Ziploc safer-sex kit. Then I close the bathroom door. Finally. Peace and quiet.

Meanwhile, back in the kit...

"Oh, my stars!" the mint one exclaims upon meeting my dental dam. "Will you look at who we have here?"

The black one says, "Well, maybe that explains why we've all been stuck in the bottom of a book bag. Miss Thing has her real gear here. And look at her trying to front. Wining and dining with alla those boys. Didn't mess wid none of 'em 'cause they're not even on the menu."

"Ha!" said the dental dam. "I wish. I got less chance than you all of seeing any action. I got a shorter shelf life. Christ! I'm not even packaged. Besides, it's not about sexual preference. She's just too damn picky."

"I was just telling Miss Thing that, wasn't I?" the black condom said.

Glancing at my watch, I see it's time to go to work. I shut off the computer and jump into the shower. While washing my hair I hear a familiar voice, smell mint on its breath. "You know, sugar, a good lookin' woman like yourself has no call to be showering alone…"

"Give it up, will you!" I say.

"Just our point," the mint one says.

Latex is on a mission.

Mergers and Acquisitions
Zane

Three months. Three long cruel months of migraine-inducing meetings and sleepless nights spent doing research. I don't know what compelled me to even agree to the madness in the first place. I take that back. I know exactly why I agreed. I did it for the recognition. I did it for the promotion. I did it for the money.

When I first started at Jones, Baker, and Kibblehouse five years ago in the Mergers and Acquisitions Department, I was the only black face anywhere in sight. Since then, a few others have started but none of them have attained my level of success.

When Charles Baker came to me and implored me to negotiate the merger with Hammonton Enterprises, my first reaction was to ask him if he had lost his damn mind. Once he assured me that a positive result would undoubtedly get me considered for the vice-president position in the department, my entire attitude changed. Michael Young had recently left to start his own e-commerce company, trying to get in on the Internet craze, so the position was wide open. Frankly, I felt I deserved it without having to prove myself any further but you can't knock the hustle so I accepted the challenge.

I knew the merger wouldn't be easy. Roy Hammonton was infamous for his shrewd business practices. The mere thought of losing the controlling reins of his corporation probably made him age ten years overnight. I spent five days reading articles and other readily available information about the man, determined to step into the initial meeting and tantalize him so much that he would hand over the keys to the kingdom without any drama. I should have known better.

As it turned out, Roy Hammonton wasn't the problem. His son Martin was the real thorn in my side. I despised him from the moment I laid eyes on him. He looked so sure of himself, so determined, so much like me. I don't like it when the playing field is even. If I can't win, then I don't want to play. That's the Lourdes Mitchell way.

The first meeting was horrid. I left the office that night and headed straight to the closest bar I could find. After four Cosmopolitan martinis and far too many sick and totally unfunny jokes from the bartender, I dragged myself outside, took a cab, went home, and passed out as soon as my head hit the pillow.

I woke up the next morning rejuvenated, focused, and more determined than ever. I set my sights on Martin and learned everything from the name of his tailor to his favorite cologne. Not because I had a personal interest in him. I'm just an avid believer that one should always know the habits of one's enemies.

The second meeting a week later was just as bad, but I refused to turn to the bottle again. Instead, I went to the gym and took three cardio-karate classes in a row. I had to limp up out of that bitch, go home, and soak in a tub of ice water. After I got out of the tub, I called on the services of my former lover Dawson. He wasn't the best lover but he gave the most hellified massages. He came over and rubbed my ass to sleep.

Three months later the agony was still in full swing. Martin had taken over the negotiations completely. Charles and the rest of the people on my side had given up as well. It was down to the two of us. The stubborn ones.

"You do realize I'll never agree to these terms?" he asked me, pacing around the conference room table for the fifty-eleventh time.

I decided to get up and stretch my legs as well. "I'll never agree to your terms either. They're ludicrous."

"I'm so sick of this."

I leered at him and issued a comeback. "I'm sick of you."

"This can't go on forever," he stated, as if I didn't already know that shit.

"Well then, agree to our terms so I can go home and get some sleep for a change."

He laughed at me, the bastard. "You really think I'm a fool, don't you?"

"If the shoe fits." I sat back down, took a manila folder off of the increasingly larger stack, and opened it. "If you come down by 5 percent, I'll convince the partners to go for it."

"You need to stop taking those ginseng tablets, Lourdes," he responded. "They're clouding your common sense. Maybe if you come up 10 percent, we can do some business."

I don't like it when people, men in particular, try to step to me like that. "I don't need the ginseng tablets to realize that I'm more of a man than you'll ever be."

"But you're a woman."

"Exactly," I replied snidely. "I'm a woman and still more of a man than you'll ever be."

He sat down across from me at the table. "Let's cut the bullshit, why don't we?"

"I was never bullshitting, Martin. I sincerely hope you haven't been wasting my time with bullshit for the past three months."

He glanced down at his watch. "It's after eight. Want to grab some dinner?"

It was my time to laugh at him. "You're not seriously asking me to have dinner with you?"

"Why not? We both have to eat."

As much as I hated to admit it, my stomach had been belting out the Battle Hymn of the Republic for about an hour. "Okay, but on one condition."

"What's that?"

"I don't like—no, scratch that—I *refuse* to discuss business while I'm eating."

He stood up and started putting on his suit jacket. "Fine. We'll discuss something else then."

I put on my blazer and headed toward the door. "Fine by me."

Martin took me to the most elegant restaurant in town, Fratelli and Sons. I was shocked when they gave us a table without a reservation. I guess the Hammonton name still held a little clout. Once the waiter took our orders, Martin wasted no time getting into my business.

"So what's your real name?"

I almost choked on my cognac. "What do you mean by that?"

"You know good and damn well your name isn't Lourdes. Sounds like something you made up, probably in law school."

He grinned at me and I wanted to puke. Not because he wasn't attractive, because he was. Six-foot-two with caramel, smooth-as-a-baby's-ass skin, long curly eyelashes, and a cinematic smile. I wanted to puke because he read my ass like a book. Until I started Harvard Law, my name was Shanika Brown. I didn't think the name sounded professional so I legally changed it.

I tried to change the subject. "You're so damn arrogant."

"And you're so damn pretty."

I almost choked again. He was up to something and I didn't like it. The next sentence out of his mouth proved me right.

"Let's play a game, Lourdes."

I chuckled. "What type of game?"

"I intimidate you, don't I?" he asked confidently.

"Intimidate?" I adjusted the napkin in my lap and took another sip of my cognac. "Nothing and nobody ever intimidates me. I know I'm the shit, I've always been the shit, and I'm always going to be the shit."

He threw his head back in laughter. "Your conceit is somewhat attractive."

"I'm not conceited. I'm simply convinced."

He reached over that table and took my hand. "So convince me to come down by 5 percent."

I yanked my hand away. "That's what I've been trying to do for the last ninety days."

"Maybe you need to consider another approach," he stated sarcastically.

My curiosity was piqued. "Another approach like what?"

He looked at me seductively and the desire in his eyes was unmistakable, almost scary. "You said before that you're more of a man than I am. Well, I'm man enough to tell you I've wanted to take you to bed since day one. That's part of the reason I've let this whole thing drag out this long."

I was speechless. I was taken off guard. I was instantly wet.

"Everyone calls you the bitch in heels but I admire your determination and aggressiveness. It mirrors my own."

"Bitch in heels?" I giggled, trying to save face. "Sounds like some of those young bucks down in the trenches have a problem with a woman of authority."

"Forget them," he said, taking my hand again. "Let's talk about me and you. I'm wondering if a woman full of so much passion about her career is just as passionate in the bedroom. Are you?"

I yanked my hand away again. "None of your damn business, Martin Hammonton. Maybe this dinner wasn't such a good idea."

"Just like I figured. I intimidate the hell out of you."

I rolled my eyes and picked up a breadstick out of the basket, wondering how long my blackened chicken over fettuccine was going to take.

"Okay, Lourdes, if I don't intimidate you, prove it."

"I don't have to prove jack shit to you," I snarled back at him.

"What kind of panties are you wearing?"

I couldn't believe his audacity, even if it was turning me on. "What do my panties have to do with anything?"

"Tell me what kind," he insisted.

I decided what the hell and answered. "Red lace with a thong back."

"Damn!" he exclaimed. "I knew you were a sexy lingerie kind of woman."

"I just like to feel feminine, that's all."

"That's amazing, since you're more of a man than me."

We shared a good laugh.

"Maybe I was a bit out of line," I readily admitted. "I was just frustrated with your tactics."

"Let me see them."

"See what?"

"Your panties."

"Are you out of your damn..."

"Your food will be out in a few moments," our waiter said, preempting the rest of my sentence. "Can I get you another round of drinks while you're waiting?"

Martin answered, "No thanks."

The waiter walked away just as I was appreciating being saved by the bell.

"So let me see them."

"Do you really expect me to stand up and show you my panties?" I asked, stunned beyond disbelief.

"No. Take them off and give them to me."

Now, normally a woman would be highly offended by such a comment, but Shanika reared her freaky head and it was on.

"Fine," I said, getting up from the table. "I'll go to the ladies' lounge and remove them."

He pulled my arm. "No, do it right here."

"Right here?"

"Yes, sit down and take them off."

I sat back down and started surveying the situation. The restaurant was packed. It was dimly lit and a long white linen tablecloth covered our table. I inched my skirt up and shimmied out of my panties. I reached down, picked them up, and then slid them across the table beside his salad fork.

Martin held them up to his nose, whiffed them like they were roses, and then put them in his inside jacket pocket.

"Satisfied now?" I asked, proud of myself for proving that he didn't intimidate me.

"Not quite."

I frowned.

"Finger yourself."

"Excuse me?" I couldn't believe that he even went there. But once again, it was turning me on big-time.

"Finger yourself and then give me your hand."

I looked around and everyone appeared to be chowing down or engrossed in intimate conversation. I rubbed my clit with the forefinger of my left hand and then held it out to Martin. He drew my entire finger into his mouth, sucked on it like a vacuum, and then expressed his approval. "Very tasty. Just like I knew you would be."

I blushed. "You've really thought about it a lot, huh?"

"Every damn night." He flashed that cinematic smile at me and I melted like chocolate. "I have an idea. Why don't I just pay the bill so we can get out of here?"

"But we haven't eaten," I protested. "I'm starving."

"I'll feed you," he quickly replied. "We can feed each other."

Martin never gave me a chance to respond. He threw a fifty on top of the breadbasket, stood up, and pulled me up from the table. We walked out of the restaurant in silence. When we got out to the curb, through the picturesque window I saw our waiter standing in front of our table holding a tray of food.

Martin unlocked the car and opened the passenger-side door for me. As I watched him walk around the front of the car, I contemplated my next move. The ramifications of my impending actions on my career could be catastrophic. By the time he got in, I had made my final decision. I wanted the dick.

He turned on some jazz music and we engaged in minimal conversation for the next twenty minutes. The next thing I knew we were pulling up to the front gates of Broadmore Hills, the Hammonton's estate.

I was a nervous wreck. "I'm not sure this is such a good idea. I thought we were going someplace else. You live with your parents?"

"No," he chuckled. "I live in the guest cottage." He took a hold of my trembling hand. "Relax. No one is going to bother us."

Images of his father walking in on us while I had a mouthful of dick ran through my mind. "Are you sure?"

"I'm positive."

He pulled up to the guardhouse. I held my head down and curtained my face with my hand while the gigantic security gates rolled open. We drove up the long, winding driveway past the main house to the guest cottage in the rear.

I jumped out of the car and made a mad dash for the front door before Martin was even out of the car. "What's your rush? You don't have a key."

"I'm just ready to get inside."

"Do I sense some intimidation?" he chided.

I didn't respond. I just zeroed in on his key going into the lock. He couldn't get the door open fast enough for me.

"Come on in," he said after the door was open and the light in the foyer was switched on. "Make yourself at home."

I walked in and was completely in awe. His place was laid the hell out. Italian leather furniture, exquisite lamps, walls covered with originals from famous African-American artists like Wak and Vanderzee. What fascinated me the most was the greenhouse attached to the back of the cottage.

"You have a green thumb?" I asked in genuine shock. "You don't seem like a plant enthusiast to me."

He looked offended. "It's relaxing. I need to do something peaceful after dealing with bitches in heels all day."

He laughed but I didn't see a damn thing funny. "You have one more time to call me out of my name."

"I have the feeling you get called out of your name a lot, *Lourdes.*" The not-so-subtle reference to my name told me everything I needed to know. Martin had obviously done an equal amount of research on me and knew my birth name was Shanika.

I went out in the greenhouse to resist the urge to slap the shit out of him. He followed me and started giving me an express course on exotic plants from around the world, pointing them out individually and giving me a brief overview of their history.

I was beginning to think the desire he professed for me at the restaurant had subsided. Until...

He grabbed my breasts from behind and started grinding his dick on my ass. I turned around and grabbed him by the neck, pulling his face down to mine so I could explore his mouth with my tongue. I had subconsciously been yearning for that tongue action for months.

He picked me up and placed me on one of the wooden tables, knocking a couple of plants to the ground. I guess they weren't as rare as he claimed them to be. Either that or my pussy was a greater priority.

It was steamy and humid in the greenhouse, which only added to my intense horniness. He lifted the bottom of my dress up and took advantage of my easily accessible, already bare crotch. Before I knew it, he was eating the living daylights out of me.

I don't think I've ever cum so quick in my life, even when I've used my twelve-inch dildo. Damn, damn, damn! When I came, my feet hit something and we were bathed in warm water from the sprinkler system overhead. It was so incredible. It was so sensual.

Martin lifted me up in the air, my legs straddled around his shoulders and his head still buried between my thighs. He carried me back into his house and laid me down on a plush rug by the gas fireplace. He must've turned it on when I was already in the greenhouse. It was blazing when we came back in.

"I'll be right back," he whispered, getting up and heading into the kitchen.

I gazed into the flames and pondered over the situation. I knew I had absolutely no business there, but dick is like oxygen. You don't miss it until it's gone and it had been out of my life for quite some time.

One thing was sure. Whatever was about to go down between Martin and me wouldn't be a one-shot deal. I think we both realized that. I wanted to confirm it, though.

When he returned from the kitchen, carrying a tray filled with a bowl of strawberries, a bottle of champagne, and two flutes, I asked him, "Where do you see this going?"

He sat the tray on the coffee table and joined me on the floor. I propped myself up on my elbows so I could stare him in the eyes. I like to read people's eyes. You can always tell if they're lying.

"Honestly?" he replied.

"Yes, honestly."

"Lourdes Mitchell or Shanika Brown or whomever you choose to be today, part of me hates the ground you walk on and the other part admires the hell out of you. All I really want is to see if you're as wild in the sack as you are out of the sack."

I took a restorative breath and searched for the right words to say. "So you know my real name?"

"Of course. You underestimated me and that was a mistake. I knew I would conquer you from the first day I stepped foot in Jones, Baker and Kibblehouse and you smirked at me like you owned the world."

"Conquer me? Man, please! I'm doing you a favor by gracing you with my presence. Not the other way around."

Martin took my hand and kissed it. "So, are you staying or going?"

"This is crazy," I blurted out. "We can't."

"Why can't we?" Martin started pulling my damp dress up over my head and I didn't resist. "Give me one logical reason why we can't be together tonight and start arguing over the merger again tomorrow."

"Like it never happened?" I asked.

He unbuttoned his shirt and let it fall off of his shoulders while he undid the buttons on his sleeves. "Yes, like it never happened."

"Listen, Martin. As long as you know this is just about sex, then…"

"Shhhhhh," Martin whispered, covering my mouth with his index finger. "Don't say another word. Just fuck me. We'll worry about the repercussions tomorrow."

Martin slipped his tongue in my mouth. I could taste my essence on his tongue. That excited me and our kiss grew deeper until we were both moaning uncontrollably. We didn't come up for air for ten minutes.

Martin stood up and unzipped his pants. I got on my knees and helped him take them off. There it was, staring me right in the face. His dick was such a scrumptious-looking specimen.

I sucked on the head of it until he threw his head back in ecstasy. Then I went for it and deep-throated the entire thing. Even when he sat back down on the floor, I wouldn't release him from my oral stronghold. Not until he exploded in my mouth and gave me the liquid candy I'd been craving.

We smeared each other with the juice from the strawberries and took turns licking it off. I figured out he was ticklish and lingered around his belly button until he couldn't take it anymore.

I climbed on top of him and contracted my pussy muscles on the shaft of his dick, taking more and more of it in until I could feel his thighs slapping up against mine as I went up and down. He poured the chilled champagne down my back and it trickled down between my ass cheeks. We both came and took a little break, basking in the glow of the fire.

We took it to the bedroom and went at each other in several different positions until the sun peeked its head over the horizon the following morning.

Martin served me breakfast in bed. Turkey bacon, grits, and scrambled eggs. The only thing a man had ever served me for breakfast was a bowl of cold cereal. I ate every drop on my plate. I was still starving from the night before.

Martin asked me to join him in the shower and I eagerly complied. He had me place my foot on the rim of the tub and spread my pussy lips so he could eat me out under the steady stream of warm water. Then he had me face the wall so he could take me from behind. I came so hard that I cried. Nothing like that had ever happened to me before.

We spent the rest of the day in bed, getting to know each other in three ways: mentally, physically, and orally. We found out that we had a hell of a lot in common. Everything from our favorite foods to our favorite music to our favorite athletes. It was a match made in heaven—or hell, depending on how you looked at it.

Our intention was to just end it right there. To go back to being enemies, but things didn't turn out like that. The sex between us was so addictive that we both knew we couldn't let it go. We ended up fucking on the conference table just about every evening before walking out of there like we despised each other. It was adventurous at first, but both of us started craving the real thing. We needed to get the merger out of the way so we could have guilt-free sex.

Martin and I decided to get together his father and the partners from my corporation for a night of beer and karaoke. Somewhere between Charles singing "Bad to the Bone," and Mr. Hammonton singing "What's Going On," they came to an agreement on the merger all by themselves.

That let Martin and me off of the hook. We didn't want to look like coconspirators because we were sleeping together. Yes, the word got out big time. It was probably the biggest water-cooler story of the decade. It didn't matter though. We were proud to announce that we were together.

In fact, Martin and I did a little merger and acquisition of our own. We got married last fall and two months ago we acquired our beautiful son, Caleb. The most stressful situation of my life ended up netting me a vice presidency *and* the man of my dreams. What more could a sistah possibly ask for?

That's What Friends Are For

Nilaja A. Montgomery

Women suck! I hate them. They're good-for-nothing low-down dirty dogs. Actually, that's a harsh thing to say, considering I am a woman and dogs are faithful. If I had any kind of sense, I'd be straight. Naw. That wouldn't work. I can't stand that whole leaving-up-the-toilet-seat thing. So now it's back to women.

Why do they piss me off? I shouldn't even say *them*. It's more like *her*. Rahiema Walker. My ex-girlfriend. Correction, make that ex-fiancée. Why is she my ex? Because she's a playaette and tried to play the wrong woman. I wasn't havin' it. You would think that after three years you could trust a bitch. But no, that hoochie was fuckin' some barely legal tramp at the high school around the corner from my apartment building. So I dumped her. And yes, I kept the ring. It's worth at least a couple of hundred. I wasn't about to walk away empty-handed. Not after all the bullshit I put up with from that worthless piece of human flesh.

So here I was, two months later, alone in my apartment getting drunk on chocolate fudge cookies, rainbow sherbet, and

Oprah. Rahiema may have treated me wrong, but I was missin' her with a fierce passion. OK, I was missin' the sex.

It had been all that and a bag of chips with dip and then some. Feel me? That woman could work me over with just her pinkie finger and those juicy kissable lips. Damn, Rahiema was one of the finest sistas I had ever laid my eyes on. She was a darker version of Toni Braxton (another woman I would give my kidney for) and twice as fine. Rahiema had skin the color of dark plums and was just as sweet when she wanted to be. That's how I prefer my women. You know the saying: The blacker the berry, the sweeter the juice. I'm surprised all my teeth didn't fall right outta my head.

I was heading for the kitchen for another refill of rainbow sherbet when my doorbell rang.

"Hey, skank. You can't call nobody?" Araina Hill, one of my three best friends, said as she came barging into my apartment. My other two friends, Daire Grant and Joi Darling, followed behind.

"We thought you done crawled up and died in this mug," Daire said. I hadn't spoken to my friends or anyone in weeks since the breakup.

"Hey, love," Joi said in her heavy British accent. She was the only Black person I had ever met who had been born and raised in England. "How are you?" she asked, hugging me.

"I'm OK," I shrugged.

"You look like shit warmed over," Araina said, smacking her gum like the tramp we all knew she was. Araina was decked out in her usual skeezuh gear: halter top and a skirt so short it showed things only a gynecologist should see. She was right, though. My apartment hadn't been cleaned in weeks. The dishes were piling up in the sink. I couldn't have even imagined what I looked like standing there in an oversized sweatshirt, cutoff jeans, and hair tied back in a ponytail.

"Leave T. T. alone," Daire said. T. T. was short for Tilo Thomas. Me.

"Thank you, Daire," I said, hugging her round body. She was the only person who called me T. T. Daire was what we called *healthy*. She had meat on her bones. She wasn't really fat, just kinda big. Like Queen Latifah. Daire gave the best hugs and was like the mother of the four of us. She was also affectionately known as Big Momma D.

"So how are you doing, Ms. Tilo?" Araina asked, plopping herself onto my couch.

"I'm hangin'." I sat between her and Joi. Daire sat on the arm of my couch.

"Have you heard from Rahiema?" Joi asked.

"No, I haven't," I said wrinkling my nose. "And I don't wanna hear from her or about her."

"Then I guess you wouldn't be interested in hearing the dish on Ms. Rahiema," Araina said.

"What dish?"

"Thought you wasn't interested."

"Bitch, you workin' a nerve."

"You must not be gettin' any," Araina said, sucking her teeth. "You hella grumpy."

"What about Rahiema?"

"The high school tramp dumped her…for a man."

"Serves her right," Joi said. "I never did like her."

"I'm not finished," Araina said, holding up a newly manicured hand. "Anyway, I was out at Zami's, you know gettin' my groove on with a fine-ass piece of woman. I go to the bathroom, do my thing, and your ex corners me just as I'm coming out."

"What did she want?"

"She wanted to know what was up with you and if you were seein' anybody," Araina said. "She wants back in."

"She has got her nerve," Daire said. "After the way she treated my girl."

"What did you tell her?" Joi asked.

"I told her you were dating this fine-ass piece of woman and had moved on," Araina said. "What could I say? That you were locked in yo' apartment cryin' over her?"

"Thank you, Araina." I hugged her. "You slut." I added.

"You my girl. I gotcha back, baby." Araina grinned. "That ain't all. So after I tell her you was taken, bitch starts hittin' on me."

"No!" Joi's eyes bugged out.

"Yes!"

"No!" Daire said.

"Yes, dammit! Y'all need to clean the wax out ya ears so you can hear a sista."

Araina looked at them in disgust.

"That is foul," Daire said. "T. T., I got peeps who will take care of Rahiema for you."

"You always got peeps you gon' get to take care of somebody," Araina said.

"That won't be necessary, D," I said.

"I should think not," Joi said. "Violence doesn't solve anything."

"Shut up, Ms. Prim and Proper," Araina said. "Violence doesn't solve anything," she said, imitating Joi's thick accent.

"Fuck you, slut." Joi gave Araina the finger.

"Speakin' of fuckin'," Daire said before Araina could come back with some flippant remark, "you gettin' any lately, T. T.?"

"No, I haven't," I said. "And I'm not interested in gettin' any."

"Oh, bullshit on me," Araina said, rolling her hazel eyes. "It's been two months, and you mean to tell us you ain't went out and snagged you some fish tacos?"

"We all ain't nymphos like you, Araina," I said. "Some of us have class."

"Class my ass," Araina said. "You need to put on one of the hoochie-mama skirts we all know you got in your closet, go out to the club, and get that punanny stroked, baby!"

"Do you always hafta be so vulgar?" I said, even though I knew she was right. It had been a while, and I was horny as fuck.

"Two months is a long time, T. T.," Daire said. "Even Joi got hooked up last week. You know what a prude she is."

"Hello. I'm sitting right here," Joi said. "And I am not a prude. I have taste, and I have standards."

"I appreciate all of your concern," I said. "I'm just not really looking to start dating anyone right now. It's too soon."

"Who the hell mentioned anything about dating?" Araina said. "I'm talkin' pure raw sex. No commitment."

"The story of Araina's life," Joi said.

"Bitch!"

"Slut!"

"Shut up, both you," Daire said. "Now let's get back to T. T.'s problem."

"What problem?"

"Your lack of a sex life, baby." Daire stood up. "We're takin' you out tonight. You gon' eat somethin' besides chocolate fudge cookies. Let's go find somethin' for you to wear."

"Didn't I let you borrow this?" Araina asked, holding up a black sheer blouse. Daire, Joi, and me were sittin' on my bed watching Araina go through my closet.

"No, that's mine."

"Can I borrow it?" Araina asked as she took off her halter top. "I got a date tomorrow. This is perfect." As usual, Araina wore no bra. There was a 99.99 percent chance she wasn't wearin' panties either.

"You are straight hoochie, Araina," Daire said, flipping through the latest issue of *Essence,* with Toni Braxton on the cover.

"Ya mama."

"I don't think so. But I do believe it was yo' mama callin' out my name last night." Daire laughed and tossed the magazine aside.

"Bitch, please," Araina rolled her eyes. "My mama's got way betta taste."

"Too bad she lost out on the looks," Joi joined in. "Look at you."

"Don't you even try comin' for me," Araina threw up her hand. "You will get dissed." She twirled around. "This is 115 percent supreme fineness, baby." Her hands rested on her hips. "Besides," Araina continued, "y'all got nerve callin' me hoochie. I'm not the one with the mirror over my bed." She pointed a long finger at me.

We looked up at the large square glass that covered half of my ceiling. That had been Rahiema's idea, her reason being, "I like to watch." My ex had been kinky.

"Someone was into the freaky-deaky," Araina said.

"Eat me," I said.

"At least you'll be able to watch," Daire said.

"Yeah," said Joi. "Instant replay."

"You and Ms. Rahiema musta had some good times up in here," Araina said. "What other nasty stuff you guys was doin'?"

"Fuck you bitches," I rolled my eyes.

"Is that an invitation?" Joi asked. Araina, Daire, and I all looked at her, shocked. "What? The British girl can't have a dirty thought?"

"We just don't expect it, prude," Araina said.

"Skank!"

"Ice princess."

"Are you two fuckin' or what?" I said. "Y'all argue like some old married-ass couple."

"You ain't got no business talkin' about somebody fuckin'," Araina said. "We know you ain't get any."

"I gets mine."

"If your lover needs double 'A' batteries, you aren't getting any," Joi said.

"Leave my girl alone," Daire said. "She can't help it if her shit's done dried up and died." She, Joi, and Araina all broke out laughing.

"My shit is still all good." I gave them the finger. "Don't make me whip it out and give you a taste."

"That definitely sounds like an invitation to me," Araina said.

"Sounds like one to me," Joi agreed. "What about you, Daire?"

"Sounds like we're gettin' invited to a party."

"I...I was just joking." I stuttered. "Y'all betta stop lookin' at me like that," I said, my friends looking like hungry horny hyenas.

"Shut up, Tilo," Araina said, pushing me onto my back. She climbed on top. "This is what you get for always havin' a big mouth."

"Besides, if you can't fuck your friends, who can you fuck?" Daire grinned.

"That's what friends are for," Joi said.

"Oh, good Goddess," I said as Araina brought her mouth down hard on mine.

That's what started it. Soon Araina was giving me kisses on the back of my neck. I shivered at the cool wetness her saliva left on my skin. Her tongue made circular motions as she crept down my back, undoing my clothes as she went. Joi soon caught on. She took my nipple in her mouth and sucked like a baby. Daire was stroking my hair. The muscle in my rectum contracted when Araina ran her tongue between my ass cheeks. She gave me a sly grin.

"Turn around," Daire whispered in my ear. I did as I was told, turning so that her chest pressed against my back. With her left hand, Daire squeezed and played with my left tit while Joi continued sucking on my other nipple. Daire reached around my waist and ran a finger over my clit. I shivered again. She stuck the pussy-drenched finger in Araina's mouth. Araina licked it dry.

"Good." Araina licked her lips.

I pulled my knees up, giving her a clear view of a wet cunt. "You know what I want now," I said, fingering myself. Araina gave me that slick grin again. I knew that when it came to sex, Araina Dawson liked it rough. I laid down on my back. Daire, who had undressed herself at some point, had her crotch bumping up against my head. Joi had stripped out of her clothes too and was sitting cross-legged, playing with herself. Araina grabbed both of my legs and forcefully spread them. She rubbed her hands together like a mad scientist about to bring her greatest creation to life. I could barely stand the wait. Araina grabbed my buttocks in her hands.

"Now, Araina," I said praying I wouldn't come right there before she even got inside. "I want it now." Squeezing my ass, she plunged. Involuntarily I sucked in a large breath as her hand curled into a ball and slammed against the walls of my cunt. I lubricated her as she fucked deeper, and I wrapped my legs around her back, pushing her farther in.

"Hey," Joi whined, "what about me? I wanna taste." Daire, Araina, and I broke out laughin'. I had never had a woman whine about not tasting my pussy.

With Daire's fingers, I spread my labia open. "Get down there, girl."

If I had known Joi Darling could work me over with just a tongue, I would have gotten it on with her years ago. My God, that woman could eat some punanny. She was lightly dancing her tongue over my clit, teasing me. I grabbed her head and tried to push her father into me. Daire was still playing with my tit, and Araina was working her mouth on my other tit. She bit me hard enough to bring a sharp pleasure gasp from my mouth. I made her kneel so that her cunt was right in front of me. I was right: She was wearing no panties under that short skirt. I slipped my finger inside her, working that little bud between her chocolate thighs. Araina worked her hips back and forth in time with the finger fucking. My room, hell, my entire apartment, filled with the sounds of sex. After a while I had lost track of who was doing what to whom. First there was Joi eating me, then Araina, then Daire, back to Araina while Daire and Joi got it on with each other. I looked up at the mirror on my ceiling. We were like beautiful black vines entwined with one another.

My friends fucked, made love, and had sex with me that day. At one point they had me on all fours doing a train on me. Each got her chance to fuck my ass and cunt. Araina even had the nerve to fuck my snatch with my own dildo! That bitch! It was fabulous. I came and came and came and came and came all over again.

After sex we curled up under the blankets. Our bodies warmed one another. As Araina, Daire, and Joi all drifted off to sleep, I kissed each one good night. This is what life was about. Friends. They were always there to lift a gal's spirit. Hey, that's what friends are for.

The Erotic Adventures
of Jim and Louella Parsons

Bertice Berry

It all started when Jim couldn't get it up. I guess I should find another way to say it, but we just country folks. That's how we put it. That was two months ago, and he been 'fraid to try ever since. Anyway, we been married for twenty-six years and have had more than our share in the love department. We youngish still; both in our fifties, and we got a lot of love left. I told Jim just that, but it didn't help none. In all our years of marriage ahead and three before, I have never seen him so upset. Jim has a lot of pride. He don't like the idea of not being able to do his business. I stopped trying to talk sense into him and did the next best thing.

Now, I had learned years before not to take stock in none of those women's magazines. Their sex tips usually included some food or saran wrap. Jim didn't like nothing too messy. He said the only thing he wants wet is me. Anyway, whenever things were tough with me and Jim, I pray that God will give me strength, make me humble and show me where I'm wrong. Then I talk to the ancestors. I talk to them like they still alive, too. I just do it in my sleep. They always know the answers.

This time I call on the women: my mama, Aunt T, and Grandma Sadie. They a hoot.

Mama say, "Hey, girl. Don't say a word. We know just why we here."

"Uh huh," Aunt T say. "Jim can't do the do."

Grandma Sadie tell them to hush. She say, "*They* men weren't too good *no* time." She say it's better to have a man who have it but lose it all the way once, than one who never lose it but only halfway does it the rest of the time.

Now I laugh. Grandma Sadie tell me that our problem is that we done got way too comfortable with each other. She say we hit it every Wednesday and sometimes on Sunday (depending on how good my fried chicken is). Until then, I didn't know about that connection, but I vow to take more time with Sunday dinner from that point on.

Mama say, "Girl, you need to spice things up a bit, fix your hair and put on a little makeup."

Mama know that I ain't into nothing too fancy, but I remind her anyway. Aunt Sadie say I need to learn some other positions. She say I got the wife and the mother part down pat, but I need to be a bit more whorish in the bedroom.

Grandma Sadie say, "Hush. Good loving ain't in no makeup, and it certainly ain't in no slutty ways. If the man want a whore, he pay one."

Grandma Sadie say the loving in the bedroom is in all the things you do before you get there. She also say me and Jim are real good to each other, better than most, but we need to find each another all over again.

I ask her what she mean, and she say, "Girl, when the last time you rubbed that man's behind?" Before I can act shocked or tell her "never," she say, "Uh huh, that's what I'm talking about. Jim knows what he got, and he thinks he knows how he likes it. What makes a man hot is making his woman hot. He thinks he knows just what to touch and how to touch it. In all the years you've been married and all the time you were sneaking before, Jim ain't had to figure out too much. He made you happy in bed because he made you happy in life. But girl, there's a lot more you should be doing."

At that point, I want to ask what, but I hear Jim getting up so I do too. I roll over and see Jim lying on his stomach. I can tell that he's feeling badly because it's Wednesday, and in the morning he's usually feeling like he want it. Most times, but not always, he gets it too. Usually, I wait for him to come to me, but this time I go to him. I rubbed Jim's behind slow and soft at first. I hear him moaning real low.

"Mmm, baby, that feels good," he say.

I rub it some more and he turn over. And I see what I haven't seen in a long time. Mr. Jim, that's what I call him, is standing at full attention. Jim so excited he can't wait to say hello to Miss Lou. That's what he call me down there, on account of my name is Louella. Jim open my legs quicker than he usually do. He ain't wait to see if I'm ready, but I don't care, seeing his joy make me too happy to say anything. As soon as Jim try to get in Miss Lou, he loses himself.

"Dammit, God dammit," he say.

"Take your time, baby," I tell him.

I start rubbing his behind some more, but Jim too shamed to try again. He mumble "sorry" and get dressed and go on to the job he has had for as long as we been married. I pray that he don't lose that too.

After he leave, I go back to sleep so I can ask Grandma Sadie what I need to do. As soon as I get there, they're waiting.

"Girl, I told you. You need to be more seductive," Aunt T was saying.

"Hush up, girl," my mama told her. "Can't you see she feels badly enough?"

"Look like to me she ain't feeling nothing at all," Aunt T said, laughing.

"Be quiet, y'all," Grandma Sadie told them. "Baby, listen and listen good. I'm gonna give you the magic you need, but you got to add the spice to it. Like I said before, you've been doing the same thing the same way for years. You need to get to know every inch of that man's body and what really makes him feel good."

I tell her I thought I did. She say Jim and me don't know what we like 'cause we ain't had it. I don't say nothing 'cause I figure she on the other side. She got to know more than I do.

She say, "Baby, what I'm gonna tell you take patience and your 'bility to follow through. You got to do just what I tell you. How you do it is up to you, though.

"Tonight," she say, looking me right in the eyes, "you and Jim sit on this bed and talk about everything you think you want to do or have done to you. It's gonna be hard, but all you can do is talk. Don't touch no matter how hard he get. Tomorrow night you can touch each other, but you can't touch it. Then, the next night you can touch it, but don't taste. Next night, taste but don't enter. Then, on the last night, get ready to go in."

That night, Jim came home tired as always. I cook him his Sunday chicken dinner, and it ain't even Sunday. Jim smile at me real sweet, but say, "Baby, I don't want to try...let's give it some time."

I tell him, "Fine. I don't want to, but I do want to talk."

I take Jim into the bedroom that I had cleaned real good. I had the bed linens changed and sprinkled my best perfume on them.

"Sit down, Jim," I say. "Now, Jim," I say, "for years we've been doing things the same, but we gonna try something new."

Jim start to tell me how tired he is, but I tell him to listen. He ain't really seen me like that, but I know he like it. I sit him on the bed and undress him real slow. I never did that before either. When I take off his pants, I let my fingers touch him real lightly, but I remember what my grandma say so I stop myself. Then I undress. Now you got to believe me when I say this. I don't think I've ever been naked in front of my man with the lights on, so all this is making him crazy. I'm not as fine as I used to be, but he didn't see with the lights on then so all he knows is now. I sit on the other side of the bed, and Jim thinks I'm asking for some.

I tell him, "Tonight, baby, we just gonna talk. Tell me what you like, and I'll tell you. Tomorrow you get to touch me, but you can't touch me now. Friday you can touch and Saturday you can touch it and taste it. Sunday, after church, if you still want to, I'll let you in."

With that, Mr. Jim came right to attention, and I was so wet I coulda slid right off my bed. Just that little bit of talk done got us hot and ready, but I know that I gotta do just what Grandma Sadie say. So I start.

"Jim," I tell him, "I love the way you moan. It's telling me that it's good. I love the way you pull my knees apart, but I wish you would stroke my thighs and play with my breasts more and my nipples. I know they ain't like they used to be, but I still got feelings. I love your kisses too, but I wish..."

This takes me a while to say, but Jim jump up and say, "What, baby? Just tell me."

Finally, I get to it. "I wish you would kiss Miss Lou. I want you to put those big lips of yours right down there. I want you to kiss it and put your tongue on it."

I was shamed to say all that, but Jim says, "Alright, baby." He was about to do it right then, but I tell him it gotta wait.

Then I say, "Jim, I need you to touch me more. I want you to put your hand on my head like you used to. And Jim, years ago you used to smack me on the behind a little. I won't mind if you do that too."

Jim sure enough was grinning. So was I. Talking about it made me want to climb on top of him and ride him to kingdom come.

"Jim," I say, "it's your turn."

Jim ain't say nothing, but I open my eyes to see his hand is holding Mr. Jim and giving himself some good love.

"Jim!" I say, "You gotta wait." I declare. I have to call him three times before he comes to.

"Oh, yeah. Okay. Sorry, babe. Seem like I kind of got lost."

"It's your turn," I say.

Jim say okay and tell me things that make me want to lose my mind. "Baby," he say in his deep voice, "I want you to act like you can't wait to get it."

"I can't," I almost yell.

"Well, sometimes it seem like you just doing your duty."

I don't say nothing 'cause I know I got something to learn. I want to talk back too.

"Tell me what you want. Say it right in my ear. I want you to tell me it's good, that it's always good. I want you to put your mouth all over me."

I'm blushing now, but I try not to show it.

"Everywhere. My chest. I got nipples too, and I want your mouth on them. Baby, I want you to put Mr. Jim in your mouth too. I want you to suck him and lick him good. I been scared to ask you for it, but we talking, ain't we?"

Jim stood up and started fondling himself again. "We gotta wait, baby?"

I say, "Yes."

"I know. I just want to show you how I want it. Is that okay?" Jim ask. He hold Mr. Jim up with one hand and start stroking slowly with the other. "Take your mouth up and down like this, baby," he say. "Start slow and then suck harder and faster. You can touch my balls, too."

That make me want to laugh, but something tell me not to. Jim tell me to suck it 'til he say he want to come. Then he want me to stand up and bend over. He say he loves taking me from behind, but he don't do it too often because it seem like I don't like it. Now I know my grandma was right because I only remember Jim doing it twice, and both times it was so good I commence to crying. Jim must've thought I was sad, and I was too old-fashioned to tell him otherwise. I'm thinking all of this and look over to find Jim done come all over himself.

"Jim, we s'posed to wait," I say. Jim kiss me like he ain't never kiss me before and goes to sleep right there in my arms.

The next day Jim wake up singing, and so do I. He calls me three times from work, something he used to do back when we just got married.

"Can't wait to touch you," he say.

"Me neither," I whisper.

That night, I undress Jim again, but this time I lay him on his stomach. I open up some baby oil I found in the back of my cupboard and pour it all over his back.

"Mmm, that's nice," he say.

I rub his shoulders and back and down to his waist. I knead his strong back like I'm making bread.

"Yes, woman," he says between strokes.

Then I pour baby oil on his behind and down between his legs. I rub his behind and slip my oily fingers between his cheeks. It must feel good because he snatches my hands and tries to take me right then.

"Not yet," I whisper in his ear.

"Oh, woman, you driving me crazy," he say.

"You don't know the half," I whisper back.

"Who are you and what have you done with my wife?" he say, laughing.

"Lay down, man, and let me finish my business."

I oil his legs and rub them hard, front and back. I touch everything but Mr. Jim. Jim trying to get me to, but he know we gotta wait.

"Alright, woman," he say, "your turn."

He lay me down and pour oil right in the crack of my behind. He rub my behind until I think I can see Jesus. I moan, and Jim moans with me. He rub everything but Miss Lou. I gotta tell the truth and shame the devil. Jim rub my feet so good I think I will die. I didn't know feet could get you so wet. He start at my feet and work his way back up. When he get to my breasts, he could have asked me to run down the street buck-naked, and I mighta done it! He rub my breasts in a way that lets me know he has done it before, but not with me. I forgive him right when the thought comes to me. I know that he wasn't getting this from me, and part of that is my fault. Besides, we been too far not to know how to forgive. Jim must've somehow felt my thoughts because he starts to cry. I tell him it's okay and hold him. We rock each other 'til we fall asleep, oily and wet.

The next day was my grocery shopping day. I got up and took a long, hot shower, fixed my hair, and put on a little makeup. Dora, who works down at the market, say, "Girl, you look like you been getting some on the side." I want to tell her to hush and that she needs salvation, but I just grin. I couldn't help it, but something about what she said makes me feel kinda proud. I push my pride back 'cause I wasn't looking to fall and say, "Thank you." That got folks whispering and I let them. We live in a small town. I know folks gonna think and say whatever they want anyway.

That night, Jim came in smiling, holding flowers, and it ain't even my birthday. This our night to touch Mr. Jim and Miss Lou, and neither one of us can wait. Now, I have always had my husband's dinner on the table for him when he gets home. With the exception of the birth of two of our five children, his meal has always been waiting. This time though, I meet him on the porch. I give him some cold, tart lemonade and kiss him right on the mouth. Miss Brown from across the street is looking, but I don't care and neither do Jim.

"We better go in," he say.

"Let her go in if she don't like what she see."

Miss Brown must've heard me 'cause she did go in, but I saw her curtain pull back and her eye peeping through. Jim sit next to me on the porch step.

"I get to touch it tonight, don't I?" he say right up next to my ear.

His hot, sticky breath on my neck make my nipples stand out at attention and my behind got real hot. Before I could answer, Jim shock me by slipping his hand up under my dress. Now it was already dark so I know Miss Brown couldn't see nothing, but all of this is new to me. I was sure surprised, but I had one for Mr. Jim too. He reach under my dress and find me naked as the day I was born. I didn't have on a stitch of underwear.

"Louella Givens," he say, calling me by my maiden name.

I grin, and Jim commence to laugh like I ain't heard in years. He pull me by the hand and take me in. We didn't make it to the bedroom though. Good thing the children are grown and moved out of town 'cause otherwise, they'd seen more than they ever wanted to know. Jim lay me down right on the living room carpet and pull my dress up over my head. He start to kiss my breasts, and I remind him that he couldn't use his mouth 'til the next day. He shook his head but said he wasn't going to argue. He grab my breast with one hand and start playing with my nipple with the other. It feel too good to be true. I didn't know my nipple had that much life left in it. Then I take one of his hands and put it down on Miss Lou.

"You full of all kinds of surprises, ain't you, woman?" Jim say.

He rub across my thighs real light for what seemed like hours. I want to scream, "Touch it, man!" but I learned the importance of patience. By the time Jim stroke the hairs on Miss Lou, how I want to skip over the next few days and get right to it. Jim stroked the inside and whispered in my ear, "I love this pussy. This is my pussy."

My husband had never talked like this to me before. Three days before I would have been shamed to hear this kind of talk coming from him, but that night I couldn't get enough. He stroked the inside of my kitty until it was hard as him. I was moaning and hollering like I was crazy. Then, when Jim stroked my spot, which by the way I wasn't aware of before then, I squirted all over the place like a man. I was shaking so hard, Jim came right through his pants.

"Woman," he said, "what have we been missing?"

I was panting hard and smiling like a madwoman. Jim carried me to bed. I felt too weak to touch anything he had, but it was okay. I slept until twelve midnight exactly and awoke to find Jim sleeping like a baby. I waited until one minute past and pulled Mr. Jim out of the slit of his PJs and commenced to sucking him the way Jim showed me. Jim must've done thought he was dreaming 'cause he was moaning something 'bout, "No, I'm married. Please don't."

He opened his eyes and saw my mouth on him. I was looking right in his eyes. His head rolled back and he let out a moan that probably made Miss Brown across the street come to attention.

"I'm coming, baby." When he said that, I climbed on top of him and rocked slowly, allowing him to come inside me. Jim arched his back and yelled, "Sweet Lord, thank you."

"Yes," I said, "I'm coming with you."

We must've both passed out 'cause when I came to, Jim was lying next to me, grinning in his sleep. He woke up and smiled and started kissing me all over. He kissed as high as possible, and as low as possible. I stood up and bent over, and we did what we both like. We made love all day long. I fell asleep in between lovemaking and I saw my ancestors.

"Girl, you was supposed to wait," Aunt T said. "You never did know how to wait."

My grandma smiled. "Girl, hush. Sometimes rules are made to be broken. Besides," she added, "y'all been waiting over twenty years to get it right."

"Thank you," I told them.

Jim must've thought I was talking to him 'cause I heard him say, "You wait—you ain't had nothin' to thank me for yet. Come here, woman. Let me taste you."

About the Authors

ETHEL MACK BALLARD is a social worker and freelance writer. She is the founder and coordinator of ZICA Creative Arts & Literary Guild and is currently working on a collection of short stories. A native of Cleveland, and a graduate of Howard University, she currently resides in Sacramento, California.

BERTICE BERRY is the author of two novels, *Redemption Song* and *The Haunting of Hip Hop,* and four works of nonfiction. She holds a Ph.D. in sociology, is a former stand-up comedian, and lives in Southern California where she is raising her sister's three children. She is currently working on her third novel.

LORI BRYANT-WOOLRIDGE is the author of the novel *Read Between the Lies* (Doubleday, 1999.) She has worked in the television broadcast industry for fifteen years and is the winner of an Emmy Award for Individual Achievement in Writing. She is the co-founder and president of Mothers Off Duty, Inc., a group committed to helping teen mothers continue their education. She lives in New Jersey where she is working on her next novel.

CHERYSSE WELCHER-CALHOUN is a writer by night and a bookstore manager by day. She has published book reviews and this is her first published short story. She lives in Oakland, California with her husband, James, her two children, Henry and D'Asia, and their cat, Neferkari. She is currently working on her first novel.

MR DANIEL is a Northern California-based writer, spoken word artist, and film and video curator and educator. She has curated visual media and performed her work throughout the San Francisco Bay Area. Her writing has appeared in *Hot & Bothered 2, Best of the Best Lesbian Erotica,* and *ISSUES: The Magazine for Lesbians of Color.*

TANANARIVE DUE is the author of *The Living Blood, The Black Rose, My Soul to Keep* and *The Between.* She collaborated on the bestselling novel, *Naked Came the Manatee.* Her short fiction is included in *Dark Matter,* an anthology of African American science fiction and fantasy. A two-time finalist for the Bram Stoker Award and the NAACP Image Award, this former *Miami Herald* columnist lives in Washington state with her husband, novelist Steven Barnes.

NIKKI GIOVANNI is the author of thirteen books of poetry spanning four decades. She is the recipient of an NAACP Image Award and holds the Langston Hughes Medal for Outstanding Poetry. She has been named woman of the year by *Mademoiselle, Ladies' Home Journal,* and *Essence* magazines. A gardener and consummate lover of the blues, she is a professor of English at Virginia Polytechnic.

KAREN JOHNSON is a well-known and prolific artist and illustrator. She has published one play and written and illustrated a children's book. She manages the San Francisco branch of Marcus Book Stores and lives in San Francisco with her husband, Greg, and their children. This is her first published erotic story.

B.P. JONES is an award-winning journalist and published author. She lives in Northern California with her husband. This is her first published erotic fiction.

PRIVATE JOY is a part-time poet and author of short stories and erotic fiction. She is a graduate of Fisk University and is currently pursuing her Master's Degree in counseling at the University of Texas at San Antonio.

AYA DE LEÓN is an artist and youth worker in Oakland, California. Her work has been published in *Essence* magazine, *Children of the Dream: Growing Up Black in America, Go, Girl!: The Black Woman's Book of Travel* and *Spooks, Spies and Private Eyes: Black Mystery, Crime and Suspense Fiction of the 20th Century*. She was a member of the San Francisco Team for the National Poetry Slam 2000.

NILAJA A. MONTGOMERY is a twenty-something African American lesbian living in Oakland, California. In addition to pursuing a career in writing, she is interested in filmmaking and photography. When she's not writing, she's working at her job in a plus size women's clothing store. It's low paying but she loves it and her coworkers.

RENÉE SWINDLE received her M.F.A. in creative writing from San Diego State University. Her bestselling novel, *Please, Please, Please*, published in 1999, was a Literary Guild featured selection and has been published in Germany and Japan. She lives in Oakland, California and is hard at work on her second novel.

ZANE is the author of *The Sex Chronicles: Shattering the Myth,* and *Addicted.* She is the webmaster of EroticaNoir.com and moderator of a monthly erotica e-zine. She lives in the Washington, D.C. metropolitan area where she is working on her next book.

About the Editor

BLANCHE RICHARDSON is the manager of the Oakland branch of Marcus Book Stores, a forty-one year old Black bookstore. She is a freelance writer and editor, a mother of one, and grandmother of two-and-a-half. She is working hard on her first novel.